PRAISE FOR THE BOOK

Some people spend so long sitting they forget they have legs.

— **THE CARTOGRAPHER OF COMFORT**

I've been checking out romance novels for thirty years, but this librarian's adventure puts all my favorite heroes to shame. Finally, a book that proves the most swoon-worthy journey is learning to fall in love with your own possibilities.

— **MRS. HENDERSON (LIBRARY PATRON)**

Fear is the beginning of wisdom. It's only when people stop being afraid that they start making truly catastrophic decisions.

— **MINIMUS**

Real explorers always know how to find each other.

— **KRIS THORNE (KIT)**

THE ATLAS OF ELSEWHERE

ADVENTURE BEGINS IN THE MARGINS

L J RIBAR

The Atlas of Elsewhere

Copyright © 2025 by L J Ribar

All rights reserved worldwide.

Published in the United States by Wine Glass Press www.WineGlassPress.com

Genres: Magical Realism/Literary Fiction, Cozy Fantasy

~

ISBN Hardback: 978-1-959078-31-9

ISBN Paperback: 978-1-959078-32-6

ISBN EBook: 978-1-959078-33-3

ISBN Audiobook: 978-1-959078-34-0

~

First Edition: October 2025

PROLOGUE: THE BOOK THAT SHOULDN'T BE THERE

The trouble with libraries, Elsie Vine had learned, was that they made promises they couldn't keep.

Every morning at seven forty-five, she unlocked the heavy oak doors of the Millbrook Public Library. The familiar scent hit her—old paper and lemon oil, mostly comforting but lately carrying something else underneath. Not decay, exactly. More like... She paused, key still in her hand. Like waiting, maybe. As if the books had gotten tired of being read the same way by the same people.

God, that sounded ridiculous even in her own head.

This morning felt different, though. As she flipped the lights—main reading room first, then reference, then the back stacks in their usual order—she could swear she heard something from the poetry section. Whispers? Pages turning?

She stopped, listened. Nothing. Just the ancient radiator starting its daily complaints and her own footsteps echoing too loud in the empty space.

Elsie had been doing this for twenty-three years. The rhythm should feel natural by now. More natural than breathing, anyway, since breathing had started feeling like work lately. She wasn't sure when that had happened. Sometime after her fortieth birthday, maybe. Or when Mrs. Chen retired and left her as the only full-time librarian. Hard to pinpoint exactly.

The morning light came through the tall windows at that perfect angle, illuminating dust motes that danced like—

Like what? Tiny prayers nobody's listening to?

She shook her head. Too much coffee yesterday, probably. Or not enough sleep. Again.

At the reference desk, she rested her hand on the worn wood where countless patrons had leaned with their endless questions. *Where can I find...? Do you have anything on...? Can you help me...?* She'd helped them all, or tried to. But standing here in the cathedral quiet, she wondered who would help her find whatever she was looking for.

If she even knew what that was, which she didn't.

Something creaked in poetry—old shelving, nothing more—but it made her glance over anyway. Half-expecting what? Someone browsing at eight in the morning? The faint scent of jasmine drifted from that direction, which made no sense. This place smelled like dust and old paper and occasionally Mrs. Patterson's too-strong perfume, not flowers.

The first patron wouldn't show up for another hour. She made her tea—Earl Grey, two sugars, same chipped mug from her second year that she really should replace but couldn't bring herself to. The chip was on the handle side where her thumb rested. It felt like a worry stone now.

The stack of returns from the overnight slot waited on her desk. She liked this part, usually. The gentle detective work of figuring out where things belonged.

Pride and Prejudice—fiction, obviously. *The Joy of Cooking*—640s, though why someone would check out a cookbook from the library when you could just look everything up online was beyond her. *A Field Guide to North American Birds*—598, natural sciences, probably for the Morrison kid's school project.

But the book at the bottom made her stop cold.

She stared at it, a chill running down her spine. After two decades, she knew every book in this collection. Could navigate the stacks blindfolded if she had to. This atlas—forest green binding with topographical lines in faded gold—had never crossed her desk before.

Yet someone had placed it exactly where she kept her personal reading. As if they knew her habits better than she knew them herself.

When she opened it, expecting hiking trails or maybe bird migration routes, her breath caught.

Maps, yes. But not of anywhere that should exist.

The first page showed an island shaped like a sleeping cat. "The Realm of Scale," read the elegant script at the top. The paper felt impossibly smooth—like glass, but warm. Almost alive. The next page revealed a city built entirely on bridges, towers connected by spiraling walkways that seemed to twist through... what? Dimensions? The paper here had a completely different texture, rough as tree bark. And was that sound she was hearing? Like cables humming in wind?

This was insane. Books didn't hum.

Page after page of impossible places. A forest where trees grew downward from a star-filled sky—these pages actually smelled like pine. A library built inside a nautilus shell that whispered when she turned the pages. A garden where the paths rearranged themselves based on the walker's mood, and she could swear she smelled dirt and crushed flowers.

At the top of each page, careful script that read like poetry:

"Here, small thoughts grow large enough to live in."

"In this place, bridges collapse under the weight of words unsaid."

The handwriting tugged at something in her memory. Like a song she'd known once and forgotten. It reminded her of summer afternoons when she was twelve, sprawled on her bedroom floor with colored pencils, drawing maps with—

Kit.

The name hit her like a physical blow. Kit something, though the years had blurred the rest of their name like watercolors in rain. Her childhood friend who'd believed maps could lead anywhere if you wanted them to badly enough. They'd spent entire afternoons drawing elaborate countries with names like "The Kingdom of Lost Socks" and "The Desert Where Homework Goes to Die."

"We'll go there someday," Kit had said once, pointing to an island they'd drawn shaped like a crescent moon. Kit had been thirteen, serious as anything. "When we're old enough to choose."

"But it's not real," Elsie had protested. Even then, too practical.

"Yet," Kit had said. "It's not real yet."

Elsie hadn't thought about Kit in years. Why now?

She flipped to the back of the book, looking for publication information. Instead, she found an inscription in blue ink:

For Kit, who taught me that the best maps don't show you where to go —they show you where you already are. Until our paths cross again. —E

Her hands started shaking. She'd never written those words. Never owned this book. But that E was formed exactly like hers, with the little flourish her second-grade teacher had tried to fix.

The atlas seemed to pulse in her hands, warm and alive, and she could swear she heard something—not music, not voices, but distant laughter mixed with rustling leaves.

The front door chimed.

"Morning, dear." Mrs. Henderson approached with her usual stack of romance novels, then paused. Her silver head tilted like a curious bird. "You look different today."

"Just tired," Elsie said automatically, her hand drifting over the atlas.

"Tired, or waiting for something?" Mrs. Henderson's smile was knowing. "Sometimes they're the same thing, aren't they?" She leaned forward. "I had the strangest dream about you last night. You were in this beautiful garden, but the paths kept changing every time you took a step."

Elsie's stomach lurched. "That's... that's an odd dream."

"Dreams usually are." Mrs. Henderson straightened, looking embarrassed. "Sorry, dear. Didn't mean to be weird first thing in the morning."

The day passed in its familiar rhythm. Questions answered, books checked out and returned. But the atlas stayed on her desk like a secret. She found herself stealing glances at the impossible maps, tracing coastlines with her finger.

Sometimes the maps seemed to trace her back.

By closing time, she'd made a decision that felt both natural and completely reckless. Instead of putting the atlas in lost-and-found, she slipped it into her canvas bag.

Just for tonight. Just to figure out where it belonged.

But as she locked up and walked into the autumn evening, amber and rose painting the sky, she wondered if the real question wasn't where the book belonged—but where it might take her.

In her bag, the atlas seemed to purr with satisfaction.

Wind chimes played somewhere in the distance, a melody she almost remembered from dreams of crescent moons and friends who believed in impossible things.

For the first time in years, Elsie felt like she might be about to find out what lay beyond the edges of the map she'd been living inside.

CHAPTER 1

THE CHAIR IN THE MAP ROOM

Elsie had always been the sort of person who read instruction manuals, followed recipes to the letter, and checked the locks twice before leaving the house. So when she found herself standing in her kitchen at eleven-thirty on a Tuesday night, holding chamomile tea in one hand and an impossible atlas in the other, she was surprised by how calm she felt.

Maybe this was what a nervous breakdown looked like. She'd always wondered.

The book lay open on her dining table, pages glowing with soft, honeyed light that definitely wasn't coming from her overhead fixture. She'd been staring at the same map for twenty minutes—the one labeled "The Chair in the Map Room"—trying to convince herself the tiny details weren't actually moving.

The map showed a circular room filled with chairs of every description. Wingbacks and recliners, kitchen stools and throne-like things, simple wooden seats and elaborate velvet contraptions that belonged in opera houses. At the center sat a figure hunched over what looked like a drafting table, sketching furiously.

"Just eye strain," Elsie murmured, taking another sip of tea. The chamomile wasn't helping. "Too much close reading."

But even as she spoke, one of the chairs—a delicate bamboo thing near the room's edge—shifted slightly to the left. Like it was making room for someone.

Elsie set down her cup too hard. Tea sloshed onto the table. Her reflection in the kitchen window looked pale and uncertain, which was pretty much how she'd looked for the past twenty years. At forty-five, she was exactly what she appeared to be: a woman who'd chosen comfort over adventure so many times that comfort had become its own kind of prison.

The memory hit without warning. Herself at twenty-two, standing in the dean's office with two job offers spread across his mahogany desk. Millbrook Public Library—safe, predictable, fifteen minutes from her apartment. Or an archivist position with a research expedition documenting disappearing languages in remote Southeast Asian villages.

"Take the weekend to decide," the dean had said.

She'd already known her answer. The practical choice. The sensible choice.

The chair instead of the door.

She'd told herself it was responsible. Mature. There would be other opportunities, she'd said. But there hadn't been—or rather, she'd stopped looking. One careful choice had led to another until careful had become a cage made of sensible cardigans and predictable days.

When had she gotten so... small?

The atlas pulsed gently, pages ruffling though there was no breeze in her kitchen. The inscription on the back caught the light: *For Kit, who taught me that the best maps don't show you where to go—they show you where you already are.*

Kit. The name pulled at something in her chest, like a fish hook in memory. She could almost see a face—laughing eyes, ink-stained fingers, someone who'd never learned to sit still. But the harder she reached for it, the more it slipped away, leaving only the taste of summer afternoons and the sound of pages turning.

"I'm losing my mind," she said aloud. Her voice held more wonder than worry, which was probably not a good sign.

She reached out to touch the page, meaning only to trace the outline of the strange room. Her fingertip barely grazed the paper when the world tilted.

The kitchen didn't disappear so much as *fold away*, like origami in reverse. One moment she was standing on familiar linoleum, surrounded by the comfortable clutter of her life, and the next she was stepping through what felt like warm honey and electric silk into—

Silence.

Not the absence of sound, but the presence of it. Deep, breathing quiet that seemed to come from the walls themselves. The air felt different here—lighter, spun from possibility instead of ordinary molecules. And warmer than it should be, given that she was apparently inside a book.

Don't think about it, she told herself. *Just... don't.*

She was in the exact room from the map. Circular, high-ceilinged, filled with more chairs than she could count. The floor was smooth stone that felt like sea glass under her feet, and the air smelled of parchment and something like cinnamon and old wood.

But it was the sound that made her breath catch—a gentle symphony of whispers, as if each chair were murmuring stories of everyone who'd ever sat in it. Love songs from rocking chairs, lullabies from nursery seats, heated arguments from kitchen stools.

The figure at the central table looked up, and Elsie's stomach lurched. Not quite human—too tall, too angular, with fingers that were slightly too long. But its face was kind, with eyes like old tea stains and a smile that suggested it had been expecting her.

"Ah," it said, setting down its pen carefully. "A visitor. It's been some time since anyone found their way here." Its voice rustled like pages being turned, with an undertone like wind chimes made from pressed flowers. "I am the Cartographer of Comfort. And you, I believe, are facing a choice."

Before Elsie could ask what the hell that meant, something small scuttled across the floor toward them. At first she thought it was a beetle, but as it got closer she saw it was more complex—part insect, part jewel, part tiny mechanical marvel. It wore what looked like a minuscule monocle and carried itself with tremendous dignity.

"Another one," it said, adjusting its monocle with one delicate leg. Its voice was like a pen scratching paper. "I suppose you're here about the chairs-versus-doors situation? It's always about the chairs-versus-doors."

"Minimus," the Cartographer said gently. "Perhaps some courtesy?"

"Oh, right. Courtesy." The beetle cleared what might have been a throat. "Welcome to The Chair Room, where every seat tells a story and most of them are tragedies. I'm Minimus, philosopher, critic, and occasional voice of reason, though I find reason is overrated in places like this." It peered up at her through its monocle. "You look like someone who's spent far too much time in sensible chairs."

Despite everything—the impossible room, the talking Cartographer, the philosophical beetle—Elsie found herself almost smiling. "You're not wrong."

"They never are," Minimus said with satisfaction. "Now then, shall we get on with the existential crisis? I have a lecture on the metaphysical implications of furniture later."

Elsie looked around at the profusion of chairs. Each one seemed to tell a story: leather armchairs worn smooth by countless evenings, kitchen stools stained with flour and tears, rocking chairs that still moved though no one sat in them.

"I don't understand," she said. "Where am I? What is this place?"

"The better question," the Cartographer said, rising with impossible grace, "is where do you want to be?" It gestured to the chairs. "Each represents a choice to stay. To remain comfortable, safe, known. There's no shame in sitting. Rest is sacred. But..."

It moved toward her, footsteps silent on the stone floor. "Some people spend so long sitting they forget they have legs."

"Metaphorically speaking," Minimus added. "Though I've seen cases where the forgetting became surprisingly literal. Very awkward."

Elsie's gaze drifted from chair to chair. The overstuffed recliner that whispered of Sunday crosswords. The office chair promising steady employment and predictable days. The church pew offering community without risk.

All of them looked comfortable. All of them looked safe.

All of them looked like her life.

"And if I don't want to sit?" she asked.

The Cartographer smiled, and its fingers gestured toward the walls. For the first time, Elsie noticed doors set between the chairs like punctuation marks. Some were grand, others simple. A few seemed made of impossible materials—one looked like compressed starlight, another like the sound of rain on leaves.

"Then you map," the Cartographer said simply. "You choose a door and see where it leads. But know this—" It moved closer, and she caught a scent like ink and distant thunder. "Once you begin mapping, you change. Every door you open changes who you are. Some people prefer to remain themselves, unchanged and unchanging."

"Terrifically boring," Minimus muttered. "Like reading the same book for seventy years and pretending it's profound."

Despite herself, Elsie was drawn to one of the chairs—a reading chair positioned between a window showing impossible stars and a small table set for tea. It would be so easy to sink into its embrace, to let the cushions cradle her while she watched other people's adventures from a safe distance.

She'd been doing that her whole life.

"The atlas," she said suddenly. "How did it get to my library?"

The Cartographer tilted its head. "Books find their way to people who need them. Perhaps someone finished their journey and left it for the next traveler. Perhaps it grew tired of waiting." Its eyes glinted. "Books aren't always as passive as they appear."

"Particularly atlases," Minimus added, polishing his monocle. "Strong opinions about destinations."

"And Kit?" The name slipped out before she could stop it.

Something flickered across the Cartographer's face. Minimus went still, monocle pausing mid-polish.

"Kit is..." the Cartographer chose words carefully, "someone who learned that maps aren't about destinations. They're about the courage to leave the chair."

"Also," Minimus said quietly, "someone who believed every story deserves to be finished, even if the ending isn't what you expected."

A memory surfaced: herself at twelve, sitting in the town library with someone whose face stayed frustratingly out of focus. Two children bent over fairy tales, making plans to find the secret door that surely existed somewhere. One of them—Kit—laughing and saying, *"When we find it, Elsie, we'll go everywhere. Every single everywhere there is."*

The memory felt real and impossible at the same time.

"I dreamed about Kit, didn't I?" she said softly. "Made them up because I was lonely."

The Cartographer moved back to its table, picking up the pen with those unnaturally long fingers. "Does it matter what Kit was? What matters is what Kit meant. What Kit taught you about the difference between maps and chairs."

"Finally," Minimus said with approval. "Someone who understands the important questions."

The Cartographer began sketching again, and Elsie realized it was drawing her—but not as she was. In the sketch, she stood straighter, eyes bright with curiosity instead of clouded with doubt. Around the figure, doors opened onto landscapes that made her heart race: a forest where books grew on trees, a city built in the curves of a shell, a garden where paths rearranged themselves based on what the walker needed to find.

"I'm scared," she admitted.

"Naturally," Minimus said. "Fear is the beginning of wisdom. It's only when people stop being afraid that they make truly catastrophic decisions."

"Fear means you're paying attention," the Cartographer agreed. "The question is: what scares you more? The journey, or staying exactly where you are for the rest of your life?"

Elsie looked around the room once more. Every chair called to her with promises of safety, predictability, the known quantity of a well-ordered life. She could feel their pull, could imagine sinking into any one of them and letting the world turn without her.

But then she thought of her library, how even the books seemed to be waiting for something more. Twenty-three years of the same routine, the same careful steps through the same careful days. Standing in that dean's office at twenty-two, choosing the safe path and watching all the other paths disappear like doors swinging shut.

And she thought of Kit—real or imagined—who'd believed that everywhere was worth exploring.

"The doors," she said, surprised by the steadiness in her voice. "How do I choose?"

The Cartographer looked up, and its smile was radiant. "You don't choose the door. The door chooses you. You simply have to be willing to walk toward it."

As if summoned, one of the doors began to glow with warm, golden light. Smaller than the others, with a simple brass handle worn smooth by countless hands. Above it, words appeared in elegant script: *The Realm of Scale*.

"Small thoughts grow large enough to live in," Elsie read aloud.

"Your first destination," the Cartographer confirmed. "Ready?"

"Is anyone ready for philosophical beetles?" Minimus asked, climbing onto her shoulder with surprising weight. "I've agreed to accompany you, by the way. Someone has to keep you from stepping on the local philosophers. They take it personally."

Elsie thought of her kitchen, her careful life, her neat apartment where everything had its place and nothing ever changed. Then she thought of the impossible atlas, warm in her hands and full of promises that had nothing to do with safety.

The door handle was warm under her palm, heated by sunlight from no earthly source. When she turned it, she felt a rush of air that tasted like honey and ink and the first day of spring, and heard something that might have been music, or laughter, or very small voices in very large debates.

"After you," Minimus said from her shoulder. "And remember—in The Realm of Scale, it's not the size of the philosopher that matters, it's the enormity of their opinions."

Elsie took a deep breath, thought once more of Kit and summer afternoons and places that existed only in the margins of possibility, and stepped through.

The sensation was like diving through liquid starlight—weightless suspension, then the gentle shock of solid ground. But the ground felt different here, each step sending tiny reverberations up through her bones, as if the earth were made of something more responsive than ordinary dirt.

Behind them, The Chair Room settled back into its breathing quiet, the Cartographer's pen scratching steadily as it added new details to endless maps. On the drafting table, Elsie's portrait smiled from the paper, and around her sketched figure, doors opened onto adventures that had only just begun.

The chairs, patient as always, continued their eternal wait.

CHAPTER 2

THE REALM OF SCALE

The first thing Elsie noticed was that her footsteps had become thunderclaps.

She froze just inside the doorway, one foot still raised, watching tiny figures scatter like dust motes across what looked like an enormous marble floor. Each shift of her weight sent vibrations rippling outward like earthquake tremors. What she'd taken for a simple step had apparently registered as a minor catastrophe.

Great. I could destroy an entire world without even trying.

"Careful!" Minimus hissed from her shoulder, his voice now the only thing that seemed normal-sized. "You nearly flattened the Philosophy Department!"

Elsie looked down—slowly, carefully—and saw that what she'd mistaken for empty floor was actually a bustling city. Tiny spires rose no higher than her ankles, connected by thread-thin bridges that hummed with almost inaudible music as microscopic figures crossed them. The whole civilization couldn't have covered more than a few square yards, yet it pulsed with activity.

The air smelled of impossibly small flowers and carried the

sound of conversations like cricket song. Somewhere in the distance, tiny bells. Or maybe laughter. Hard to tell.

"Sorry," she whispered, though even her quietest voice boomed across the miniature landscape. Several tiny inhabitants looked up at her with what seemed like polite interest rather than terror.

They're not afraid of me, she realized. *They're curious.*

"Don't apologize," Minimus said dryly. "They'll debate the philosophical implications of your regret for six hours. Inch-High Philosophers aren't known for brevity."

"Six hours?" Panic fluttered in her chest. How long had she been gone? Would anyone notice? But even as the worry formed, she couldn't quite remember what day it had been when she'd opened the atlas. The normal world felt distant, like a dream half-remembered.

"Time works differently here," Minimus said, apparently reading her thoughts. "Stop trying to measure it by your old standards."

"Did you just—"

"I'm a well-read beetle. Deal with it."

A group of tiny figures began making their way toward her feet. They moved with the dignity of beings who considered themselves far larger than they appeared. As they got closer, she could see elaborate robes made from flower petals and spider silk, each garment catching light like stained glass.

The leader—distinguished by an impressive beard that looked like it was woven from dandelion fluff—raised his voice in what was presumably a shout but sounded like grass whispering in breeze.

"High Philosopher Threadbeard extends greetings," Minimus translated, adjusting his monocle. "He formally requests a Colloquium of Scale. Says your arrival raises important questions about perspective and the relativity of size."

"A what now?" Elsie asked, kneeling carefully. The marble was cool against her knees, and the motion still made several philosophers steady themselves, but they seemed more intrigued than alarmed.

"A debate. They love debates. They've been having the same one about the fundamental nature of existence for three hundred years. Quite proud of it."

Three hundred years. The idea both fascinated and unsettled her. In her world, that might be called obsession. Here, it seemed like devotion.

More philosophers were gathering, emerging from doorways and descending from bridges no thicker than her eyelashes. They arranged themselves in a neat semicircle, voices rising in harmonious humming that sounded like bees discussing advanced mathematics.

"They want to know," Minimus continued, "whether you experience yourself as large, or whether you just exist in a realm where everything else is small. Also, whether largeness is inherent or contextual. Also, whether measurement itself isn't just a construct that—"

"Oh," Elsie interrupted, watching more philosophers join the group, some riding what appeared to be domesticated ladybugs. "This could take forever."

"If you let them. But here's the thing—they ask the right questions even when they never find answers. Question is: what are they helping *you* understand?"

Elsie paused. *What am I learning?* She studied the gathered philosophers, noting how they stood with perfect confidence despite being tiny, how they engaged with ideas that seemed too large for their physical forms.

One philosopher—wearing what looked like a cape made from a single autumn leaf—stepped forward and delivered what sounded like an impassioned speech. The leaf caught light and threw tiny shadows that danced across the marble.

Minimus listened intently. "Professor Leafcloak argues that your presence proves multiple scales of reality operating simultaneously. However, Dr. Pebblestone—" he indicated another philosopher shaking a twig topped with a crystal "—contends that size is just an illusion created by limited perspective."

Am I the right size? The question hit unexpectedly. For so long she'd felt too small for her own life—too small for adventure, too small for risk, too small for anything but safe routines and solitary evenings. But what if she'd been exactly the right size all along?

"What do they want me to say?" she asked.

"Wrong question," Minimus replied, gentler now. "Right question is: what do *you* want to say? What does their debate make you think about scale?"

Elsie found herself charmed by the philosophers' earnestness, but also challenged. Here were beings who could be swept away by a sneeze, yet they spoke of existence with the confidence of giants. Their size hadn't diminished their sense of importance.

"I think," she said carefully, "that size might be about what you're measuring against."

The philosophers fell silent, tiny faces turned up with rapt attention. In the quiet, she could hear her heartbeat and air moving through the miniature cityscape.

"You're small compared to me," Elsie continued, something loosening in her chest, "but I suspect your thoughts and feelings are exactly as large as they need to be. And compared to the universe, I'm incredibly tiny, but I don't usually feel that way because I'm not standing next to galaxies."

But I have been measuring myself against the wrong things. Other people's adventures instead of my own capacity. Measuring my worth by the size of my world instead of how deeply I engage with it.

Professor Leafcloak delivered enthusiastic commentary while Dr. Pebblestone raised counter-points that sparked immediate discussion. Their voices created gentle cacophony, like wind chimes made of whispers.

"They're quite taken with your theory," Minimus reported. "Though now they're debating whether thoughts can have measurable size, and if so, whether a small being thinking large thoughts actually becomes larger."

"Oh dear," Elsie said, but she was smiling. "Hope I haven't made things complicated."

"You haven't made anything complicated. You've recognized something that was already true. Question is: what are you going to do with that when you return to your normal-sized world?"

The weight of the question settled over her. *What would she do?* Could she carry this sense of appropriate scale back to her library, her apartment, her carefully circumscribed life? Could she remember that her kindness was exactly the right size, even if her world felt small?

She looked down at the bustling community, each philosopher perfectly sized for their existence, each engaged in pursuits that felt monumentally important despite their miniature scale. She'd spent so much time feeling small—small in her job, small in her apartment—that she'd forgotten to notice what was actually the right size.

Her knowledge of books. Her capacity to help people find what they needed. Her gift for listening, for creating safe spaces. These hadn't been too small. They'd been exactly what they needed to be.

Her sense of possibility had shrunk.

"I think I understand," she said softly. "It's not about how large you are. It's about how large you're willing to become."

The philosophers erupted in delighted chaos, tiny voices rising in celebration. Several immediately began constructing miniature podiums while others rushed off to fetch colleagues. The sound was like enthusiastic sparrows discovering berries.

Minimus chuckled—sand shifting in an hourglass. "Congratulations. You've just provided them with material for another century."

As if responding to their excitement, the realm began to shimmer. The marble remained, but new details emerged: tiny gardens where flowers grew no taller than grass, libraries with postage-stamp books that glowed with inner light, theaters where dust-mote audiences applauded performances on thimble-sized stages. A complete world, perfectly scaled to its inhabitants, lacking nothing except recognition that it was sufficient.

Like my library. Complete in itself, but I kept wishing it were something else.

"Before we go," Minimus said, settling more comfortably on her shoulder, "what did you learn that you can take with you?"

Elsie watched the philosophers continue their animated discussions. "That scale is contextual. That being the right size for your life matters more than being the size you think you should be."

"And?"

"That thinking large thoughts might actually make you larger."

"Good. Hold onto that. You'll need it next."

She closed her eyes, letting her mind drift to the atlas, its pages full of impossible places and promises of transformation. She thought about Kit—whoever Kit was—and the inscription about journeys being about discovering territories of the self.

When she opened her eyes, a new door had appeared at the realm's edge. Larger than the simple portal from The Chair Room, it seemed made of something that shifted between solid matter and pure emotion. The surface rippled like water, but when she looked closely, she could see faces—expressions of joy, sorrow, fear, hope, flowing together endlessly.

Above it, words wrote themselves: *The Realm of Emotion.*

"Reality responds to emotional states," she read aloud.

"Ah," Minimus said, suddenly more serious. "That's a realm requiring careful navigation. Emotions reshape the very ground you walk on. Ready for that level of instability?"

Elsie waved goodbye to the philosophers, who managed distracted waves with tiny staffs before returning to what appeared to be construction of an even more elaborate debating platform. High Philosopher Threadbeard had produced a scroll barely visible to her naked eye and was preparing another lecture.

"Will they be okay without us?" she asked.

"They've been arguing since before I was assembled. They can manage. Question is whether we can manage what's next. In the Realm of Emotion, you won't have the luxury of observing from a distance. Everything you feel becomes real around you."

Elsie paused with her hand on the door handle, which felt warm and pulsed gently like a heartbeat. Through the rippling surface, she glimpsed landscapes that shifted with flowing emotions—gardens that bloomed and withered with love and loss, mountains that grew with pride and crumbled with despair.

"What if I feel something wrong?"

"No wrong feelings," Minimus said, but his voice carried warning. "Only feelings that are more or less useful. The trick is acknowledging them without being overwhelmed. And remember—you learned something important about scale. Your feelings don't have to be larger than you are."

"That sounds like something Kit would say," Elsie murmured, surprised by her own words.

"Perhaps. Or perhaps it's something you've always known, and Kit was the part of yourself that remembered it."

The door opened before she could puzzle through that, revealing space that defied description. Not darkness, but absence waiting to be filled—like canvas before the first brushstroke, silence before the first note. As she stepped through, she felt reality holding its breath, waiting to see what she'd make of it.

This is where things get interesting, she thought, and immediately felt the space respond to her anticipation, walls materializing from hope and curiosity, floor solidifying from determination mixed with carefully managed fear.

Behind them, The Realm of Scale continued its eternal debates, perfectly content in miniature completeness, while ahead, something more volatile waited to be discovered.

The philosophers' voices faded to whisper, then silence, but their lesson lingered: sometimes the most profound changes happened not by becoming larger, but by recognizing you'd been exactly the right size all along—and having courage to think thoughts large enough to match your true potential.

Now came the test of whether that knowledge would hold when reality itself began bending around her feelings.

INTERLUDE #1: LETTER TO KIT

Written on paper that appears to be regular library stationery, though it seems unusually small, as if sized for someone writing from a miniature desk

Dear Kit (if you're real),

I'm writing this sitting at what I can only describe as a teacup-sized desk, though that makes it sound charming rather than deeply unsettling. Everything here is small—not just physically small, but conceptually small, as if big thoughts have been compressed until they fit into spaces no larger than thumbtacks.

God, this is insane. I'm writing letters to someone who might not exist from a place that definitely shouldn't exist.

I keep thinking you would have loved this place. Or maybe you would have hated it. I'm not sure anymore what you would think about anything, because I'm not sure anymore whether you ever thought anything at all.

Did you exist, Kit? Were you a real person who sat across from me in the library, planning adventures to impossible places? Or are you something my loneliness created—the perfect friend who understood my hunger for magic because they were made of the same hunger?

Because if I made you up, what does that say about me? That I was so desperate for connection I invented an entire person?

If you were real, did you ever feel overwhelmed by the scale of everything? Not just the physical bigness of the world, but the enormity of all the choices we have to make, all the ways we can disappoint ourselves and others? Did you ever feel so small that you wondered if your dreams mattered at all?

The philosophers here (yes, there are philosophers, and they're exactly as argumentative as you'd expect) spend all their time debating the nature of size and significance. They're no bigger than dust motes, yet they speak of existence and meaning with complete authority. It makes me think that maybe size isn't about physical dimensions at all. Maybe it's about what you're willing to believe about yourself.

I've spent so many years feeling small, Kit. Small in my job, small in my apartment, small in my carefully managed life. But watching these tiny beings treat their miniature debates as if they contained the secrets of the universe, I'm starting to wonder if I've been measuring myself against the wrong things.

Or maybe I'm having a complete breakdown and this is all elaborate wish fulfillment. Maybe I'm actually sitting in my library having a psychotic episode.

If you were real, what would you say about that? Would you tell me I was always exactly the right size for my own life? Would you remind me that the girl who dreamed of exploring impossible places was never small at all—she just let other people convince her that her dreams were too big?

I don't know why I'm writing to you. If you're real, you probably don't remember a quiet girl who was too afraid to write letters. If you're not real, then this is just another conversation with myself, another way of avoiding the harder question of who I am when I'm not pretending to be practical.

But here's what I've learned from the dust-mote philosophers: sometimes the act of speaking as if something matters makes it matter. Sometimes treating a question as important is what gives it importance.

So I'm going to assume you're real, at least for the length of this letter. I'm going to assume that somewhere, you're living the kind of life we dreamed about—full of adventures and discoveries and moments that make ordinary Tuesday afternoons feel like chapters in an epic story.

And I'm going to assume that if you could write back, you'd tell me what you always told me: that the best adventures begin when you stop worrying about being ready and start being willing to take the first step.

Your possibly imaginary friend, Elsie

P.S. - The strangest thing happened today. For just a moment, while listening to the philosophers debate the relativity of significance, I could swear I heard someone laughing in the distance. It sounded exactly like you used to sound when you had figured out the answer to a puzzle I was still struggling with. If that was you, somehow, then I hope you're proud of me for finally learning that small thoughts can grow large enough to live in.

CHAPTER 3

THE REALM OF EMOTION

The first thing that dissolved was the ground.

Not all at once—that might have been easier. Instead, the solid surface beneath Elsie's feet began to soften like ice cream in sunlight, responding to her spike of anxiety about walking into a realm where feelings had physical form. Her knees locked as she felt herself sinking, hands reaching for stability that didn't exist. The more worried she got about the dissolving ground, the more liquid it became, until she was ankle-deep in what felt like warm honey mixed with uncertainty.

This is insane. This can't be happening.

"Stop thinking about it," Minimus advised from her shoulder, claws gripping her cardigan tighter. "The realm responds to emotional states, not logical ones. Fear makes things unstable. Try thinking about something solid."

"Like what?" Elsie asked, her voice tight as her feet sank deeper. She could feel her heart hammering, embarrassment heating her cheeks as she realized how quickly she'd lost control.

"Something that makes you feel grounded. Literally."

Elsie closed her eyes and thought about her library—books in her hands, solid and reassuring, the familiar resistance as she shelved them. The worn oak of the circulation desk, smooth from decades of hands. The dependable stone foundations. Her pulse slowed, shoulders dropping, and the ground firmed beneath her feet into something like warm sand mixed with well-worn leather.

When she opened her eyes, she was standing in a landscape that defied every natural law but somehow made perfect emotional sense. The sky wasn't blue but the color of contentment—a warm, golden shade that pulsed gently with her heartbeat. Hills rolled away in every direction, colors shifting with her mood: green where she felt curious, purple where uncertainty lingered, silver where wonder touched her thoughts.

The air felt different against her skin—lighter, as if it were spun from possibility rather than ordinary molecules. When she breathed it in, it tasted of honey and starlight, with an underlying effervescence that made her slightly dizzy.

"Remarkable," she breathed, and the word itself seemed to shimmer in the air before settling into the landscape like dew, creating tiny crystalline formations that chimed softly.

"Careful with the amazement," Minimus warned. "Wonder is lovely, but too much makes the terrain unstable. I once knew a traveler who got so excited about a sunset they accidentally created a volcano."

As if to prove his point, a small hill in the distance began to glow brighter as Elsie's fascination grew, its peak starting to smoke suspiciously. She could hear low rumbling, like distant thunder.

She took a deep breath, consciously relaxing her shoulders— habits from years of managing stressed library patrons. "How do I... moderate this?"

"Practice," came a new voice, warm and melodious with an undertone like distant thunder. The sound seemed to come from everywhere at once, vibrating through the ground into her feet, up her spine where it settled like a gentle headache made of music.

Elsie turned to find a being that seemed made of shifting

emotions themselves. One moment it appeared solid and human-shaped, the next it flowed like water or flickered like flame, edges always slightly out of focus as if she were looking through tears.

"I am Sym," it said, its voice carrying the weight of every feeling Elsie had ever tried to name but couldn't quite capture—the ache of music almost too beautiful to bear. The hollow satisfaction of finishing a meaningless task. The particular loneliness of being surrounded by people who couldn't see you clearly.

"I shape tools from emotions, and I've been waiting for someone who needs to learn the difference between feeling something and being overwhelmed by it."

"Tools from emotions?" Elsie asked, watching as Sym's form solidified into something more consistently human-shaped, though its edges still shimmered. The air around it smelled of heated metal and sea salt, with underlying sweetness like overripe fruit.

In response, Sym reached into what might have been a pocket or a fold in space, withdrawing something that looked like a compass. The metal was warm, humming with a frequency she could feel in her fillings. Instead of pointing north, its needle swung toward whatever emotion was strongest, and instead of directions, the face was marked with feelings: Joy, Sorrow, Anger, Fear, Love, Wonder, and dozens of others in script that shifted based on what was needed.

"An emotional compass," Sym explained. "Useful for travelers who need to navigate by feeling rather than geography. It doesn't tell you how to feel—it tells you what you're already feeling, which is the first step toward understanding why."

The compass needle swung toward Elsie, stopping at "Curious Apprehension"—a feeling she recognized but had never had words for. The precision made her laugh, a sound that surprised her and caused small flowers to bloom around her feet.

"But this isn't for you," Sym continued, tucking the compass away. "Not yet. You're not ready for such a tool."

Elsie felt her jaw tighten, that old familiar response to being dismissed. But instead of swallowing the reaction, she let herself notice it. The irritation sat in her throat like a small coal, warming her voice. "What do I need to be ready?"

The landscape around her feet solidified in response to her assertiveness, taking on the texture of well-packed earth rather than uncertain sand. She could feel the change through her soles, sudden stability that made her stand straighter.

Sym's form shimmered with what might have been approval, sending ripples of warmth across the landscape. "You need to understand that emotions aren't weather—they're not things that happen to you. They're information. They're fuel. They're tools you can learn to use consciously."

As if to demonstrate, Sym's form shifted, becoming more solid. Around them, the landscape responded by becoming clearer, more stable, colors more vivid. "Fear," Sym said, and a brief shadow passed over the golden sky, bringing a cool breeze that made Elsie shiver, "can be a warning system that points toward what matters most."

The shadow created valleys that clearly delineated safe paths from dangerous ones, edges so sharp she could see exactly where to step.

"Anger," Sym continued, and heat rose in the air, making her skin prickle, "can be fuel for necessary change, the energy that says 'this situation requires action.'"

Red flush built bridges over obstacles that had seemed impassable, solid structures that rang like bells in the wind.

"Sadness," and the air grew thick and moist, carrying the scent of rich earth, "can be compost from which new growth springs, honoring what was valuable about what you're leaving behind."

Blue wash enriched the soil until new plants sprouted spontaneously, leaves unfurling with sounds like whispered secrets.

"But only if you learn to work with them instead of being worked by them. Most people spend their lives either avoiding emotions or drowning in them. Neither approach serves growth."

Elsie thought about her library life, how she'd spent years trying to avoid strong feelings altogether. Keeping things pleasant, manageable, safe. The landscape grew flatter, more beige, reflecting her habit of emotional dampening. Even the air seemed thinner, less nourishing.

Her throat tightened. "I think I've been afraid of feeling too much."

"And what has that fear cost you?" Sym asked gently, its form becoming more present. The question seemed to hang in the air with visible weight.

Elsie found herself thinking not just with her mind but with her whole body. Her stomach clenched as uncomfortable memories surfaced. Shoulders drew up as she remembered opportunities declined. Hands clenched as she considered the price of her careful life.

The emotional landscape began to shift, responding to complicated feelings. The terrain painted itself in colors that had no names but somehow expressed exactly what regret felt like, what missed chances looked like, what unlived possibilities sounded like in the dark.

She saw herself at twenty-five, standing in an office that smelled of leather and old books, two job offers spread across mahogany. Her hands had been shaking as she held the letter from Prague—a position at the National Library, working with medieval manuscripts, traveling to monastery libraries across Europe to document illuminated texts slowly crumbling away.

She could still feel that letter's weight, how her pulse had quickened reading about research opportunities that would have changed everything. But Prague had felt so far from everything familiar, so full of unknowns. Her chest had tightened just thinking about navigating a foreign city, stumbling through Czech conversations, making mistakes in front of judging colleagues.

The realm showed her the ghost of that choice now: cobblestone streets she'd never walked, worn smooth by centuries. The particular echo voices made in vaulted library halls. The smell of ancient parchment and cool touch of manuscript pages that had survived wars and revolutions. She saw herself moving through that world with growing confidence, speaking three languages, hands steady as she photographed texts few people would ever see.

The phantom Elsie looked back across the years with eyes that held no accusation, only wistful understanding. Then the vision faded like smoke, leaving only faint scent of old paper and distant bells.

"I was so afraid of not being good enough," she said, voice catching. "Of failing in a foreign place where I didn't know the customs or speak the language well enough."

THE LANDSCAPE SHOWED HER MORE. She felt phantom weight of conference name tags, the particular nervousness of presenting work to strangers, how her palms had sweated when interesting people approached afterward.

She saw herself at thirty-three, at a Boston conference. Her presentation had gone better than expected—people had laughed at her jokes, nodded at her insights about rural library outreach. Afterward, a charming Seattle librarian had approached, eyes kind behind wire-rimmed glasses, genuine interest as he asked questions that showed he'd really listened.

"Would you like to continue this conversation over dinner?" he'd asked. "Maybe explore the city tomorrow if you're free?"

She'd felt her heart skip in a way both terrifying and wonderful. But her throat had closed, smile becoming automatic as fear flooded her system. The familiar cascade of what-ifs: What if they liked each other too much? What if they didn't? What if she had to open herself to love and all its risks of heartbreak and disappointment and the terrible vulnerability of being truly known?

"I have an early flight," she'd lied, watching the light dim in his eyes as he accepted her excuse with gracious disappointment.

The landscape painted the echo of that refused evening: laughter over wine that would have loosened her tongue, conversations stretching until dawn about books and dreams, walks along the harbor with someone who understood her passion for connecting people with stories they didn't know they needed.

The vision was so real she could taste salt air, feel the particular warmth of being truly seen. Her chest ached with physical longing for the life she'd refused to risk.

"I convinced myself I was being sensible," she said, voice small. "But I was just scared."

The realm showed her a hundred more moments. The writing group she'd wanted to join but decided she wasn't creative enough for—nervous flutter when she'd seen the announcement, hands trembling as she'd started to write an inquiry email and deleted it. The master's program that had offered her a fellowship—she remembered that acceptance letter's exact weight, how her breath had caught, followed immediately by familiar chest tightness that meant she was already finding reasons to say no.

Each unlived possibility created geographic features: mountains of missed connection, rivers of unexplored creativity singing in unknown languages, forests of unchosen adventures thick with possibility.

"Oh," she breathed, and the word carried such recognition it caused a small earthquake, reshaping hills and valleys around her realization. She felt the tremor through her bones.

"Yes," Sym said softly, form becoming more solid as Elsie's understanding deepened. "The cost of avoiding pain is often losing joy. The cost of avoiding risk is often losing transformation. But look again—what else do you see?"

Elsie looked more carefully at the landscape of her unlived life, blinking away tears. Slowly she began to notice something else woven through those ghostly possibilities—golden threads that caught light and hummed with their own frequency.

In each scenario, there had been a moment of choice—not just the choice to decline, but an earlier choice to even consider the opportunity. She'd been offered Prague because her work was excellent. The Seattle librarian had approached because her presentation had been engaging. She'd been invited to the writing group because someone had recognized creativity she'd barely acknowledged.

Her spine straightened as understanding crystallized, breathing deepening as something loosened in her chest. "I see..." she began, then paused as realization settled into her bones like warmth after being cold. "I see that even in choosing safety, I was someone worth choosing. The opportunities came because of who I already was, not who I thought I needed to become."

The landscape shifted again, and now she could see golden threads running through all those phantom possibilities—the same qualities that had drawn people in roads not taken were still present in the road she had chosen. Her kindness, her deep knowledge, her ability to help people find what they were looking for even when they couldn't articulate it.

"And what does that tell you about choice?" Sym asked, pulling new tools from that impossible pocket. This time it withdrew what looked like a small mirror, but its surface showed not her reflection but the emotional weather currently swirling around her—purple clouds shot through with silver threads, deep blue oceans that seemed both vast and navigable, little sparks of golden light growing brighter.

"It tells me that every moment is a new choice," she said slowly, voice growing stronger. She could feel the truth resonating in her chest, vibration that seemed to tune her whole body to a new frequency. "That I can honor what I was afraid of without being paralyzed by it. That the same person who chose safety can choose adventure."

"Now you're learning," Sym said, form radiating satisfaction that painted nearby flowers in shades of pride and accomplishment.

As if summoned, the landscape began to shift more dramatically. A path appeared, winding through terrain that would clearly test her newfound emotional awareness. She could see stretches glowing with warm colors of joy and confidence, but also sections shrouded in purple mists of doubt, dark valleys whispering of old griefs, steep climbs requiring determination's fuel.

The path pulsed with invitation, calling to her through her soles.

"What kind of practice?" Elsie asked, accepting the emotional mirror and tucking it carefully beside the atlas. The mirror was warm, and she could feel it continuing to work through fabric, gentle vibration keeping her aware of shifting emotional states.

"The realm will present situations that evoke strong emotions," Sym explained. "Your task is to use feelings as information rather than letting them use you. Think of it as learning to sail: you don't control the wind, but you can learn to work with it."

They began walking, and immediately Elsie understood what Sym meant. The ground responded to every emotional shift: when she felt confident, it became comfortable, springy surface that made walking a joy, each step releasing puffs that smelled like fresh bread and morning coffee. When doubt crept in, the path turned treacherous, surface becoming slippery, forcing her to slow down and pay attention.

But instead of suppressing doubt, she experimented with Sym's teachings. She let herself feel it fully—the tight sensation in her chest, shallow breathing, familiar urge to turn back. But instead of fighting it, she listened to what it was trying to tell her.

The doubt wasn't trying to sabotage her—it was pointing toward what mattered. She was afraid of failing not because she was weak, but because succeeding had become important. Fear was information about her values, not a character defect.

When she acknowledged doubt instead of fighting it, something interesting happened: the treacherous path didn't become easy, but it became navigable. Her feet found purchase on surfaces that had seemed impossible. Uncertainty remained, but transformed from obstacle into alert awareness that helped her choose steps more carefully.

They walked through a grove where trees grew taller or shorter based on her confidence levels, leaves rustling like applause when she felt proud and sighing like disappointment when she doubted. She learned to find middle ground—not arrogant confidence that made trees grow so tall she couldn't see sky, but steady self-trust that kept them at comfortable height.

They crossed a bridge that solidified under her feet as she chose to trust it despite fear of heights. She could actually feel the bridge becoming more real as trust increased, phantom structure gaining substance with each step. By the middle, it was solid enough to lean on railings and look down without fear.

Each challenge taught her something new about feelings' geography. Anger could be channeled into determination that literally moved mountains—or reshaped them into climbable formations. Heat flowed through her arms and legs like liquid strength. Sadness seemed to water ground so new paths appeared, tears creating streams that carved beautiful routes.

Even anxiety, when she listened to what it was trying to tell her, became an early warning system that helped her prepare for challenges before they became overwhelming. Nervous energy became useful hyperawareness that helped her notice details, readiness that prepared her for quick reactions.

The most surprising lesson came when they encountered what looked like an impassable chasm filled with thick, gray fog. The sight made her stomach drop, not with fear but with recognition.

"What is that?" Elsie asked, though she already understood.

"Numbness," Sym said simply, voice taking on new depths that made her ribcage vibrate. "The place people retreat to when emotions become too much. Many travelers try to cross by avoiding it entirely, but that only makes the chasm wider."

Elsie looked down into the gray void and felt her whole body remember it—the particular emptiness of feeling nothing at all, how her limbs had felt heavy and disconnected during years when she'd chosen not to feel rather than risk being hurt. How many years had she spent in exactly this emotional nowhere? Not happy, not sad, not excited, not afraid—just existing in careful middle ground where nothing could touch her deeply enough to hurt, but nothing could inspire her either.

Her throat tightened as she remembered that grayness's weight, how it had settled into her bones like chronic ache she'd learned to ignore.

"How do I cross without falling in?"

"You don't cross it. You acknowledge it. Numbness serves a purpose—protection when emotional weather becomes too intense to navigate. But like any tool, it becomes a problem when you use it all the time."

Instead of trying to leap over or find a way around, Elsie sat at its edge, legs folding beneath her. She looked honestly into the gray fog, letting her body remember what it had felt like to live in that emotional nowhere.

The fog seemed to recognize her, reaching up with tendrils that felt familiar—not unpleasant, just empty. Safe. Predictable.

"Thank you," she said to the fog, surprising herself with how much she meant it. "You kept me safe when I needed to be safe. You helped me survive when everything felt too much."

The fog shimmered, and she caught glimpses of younger self who had first learned to retreat into numbness. Sixteen and heartbroken over Kit's departure—though memory remained vague, she could feel that loss's weight, how it had threatened to drown her. Twenty-two and overwhelmed by first real job's responsibility, learning to dampen reactions so she could function competently.

Her chest ached with sympathy for those younger selves, who had done the best they could with available tools.

"But I don't need that protection anymore," she continued, and as she spoke, fog began to thin. She could feel the truth settling into her bones, warm certainty that made her spine straighter. "I'm learning to work with feelings instead of hiding from them."

The chasm didn't disappear, but transformed into something crossable—a narrow stream filled with clear, quiet water that reflected her face. She could still choose numbness if needed, but now it was a conscious tool rather than automatic retreat.

When she stood up, her legs felt strong beneath her, steady and ready.

By the time they reached the hilltop where another doorway waited, Elsie felt fundamentally different. Not emotionally numb, as she had been for years, but emotionally literate—able to read her own heart's language and use it as a compass. Her body felt more alive, more present, as if she'd been living in muted colors and suddenly everything had been turned to full brightness.

The new door glowed with warm, amber light that felt like sunset and honey combined, and above it appeared words she now recognized: *The Feast of Memory*.

"Ready for the next lesson?" Minimus asked from her shoulder, tiny weight somehow comforting.

Elsie checked the emotional mirror one more time, marveling at what she saw. Her anticipation flowed in golden streams that pulsed with her heartbeat. Her courage burned as steady silver light that made her stand taller. Her growing self-trust created warm, steady glow that illuminated everything around it.

But there were other colors too: threads of grief for lost time, sparks of anger at herself for playing small so long, wisps of uncertainty about what lay ahead. Instead of alarming her, this emotional complexity felt like richness, like a symphony with many instruments rather than the single, muted note she'd been living to for years.

"Yes," she said, and the word resonated through her whole body, making her fingertips tingle and heart beat stronger. "I think I'm ready to remember."

As her hand touched the door handle—warm brass that seemed to pulse with its own heartbeat—she heard something that might have been Kit's laughter, carried on wind that tasted of summer afternoons and impossible adventures. The sound filled her with joy so pure it caused flowers to bloom spontaneously around the doorway, petals shimmering with colors that expressed exactly what it felt like to choose courage over safety, growth over stagnation, the unknown over the predictably small.

The door opened onto the scent of memory fruit and promise of reclaimed possibilities, and Elsie stepped through carrying not just the tools she'd gathered, but knowledge that she had always been someone worth choosing—by others, and most importantly, by herself.

INTERLUDE #2: LETTER TO KIT

Written on paper that seems to shift color subtly as emotions change, the handwriting occasionally wavering as if the writer's feelings were directly affecting the pen

Dear Kit,

My hands are shaking as I write this. Not from cold or fear exactly, but from something I can only describe as emotional overwhelm. I've just spent time in a place where feelings become landscape, where the very ground beneath your feet responds to what you're experiencing. It's terrifying and wonderful and I keep feeling like I'm losing myself and finding myself at exactly the same time.

What is happening to me? This can't be real. But it feels more real than anything I've experienced in decades.

I'm afraid, Kit. Afraid of who I'm becoming, afraid of who I've been, afraid that if I keep changing I won't recognize myself anymore. But I'm also afraid of staying the same, of going back to the careful, contained life I built to keep myself safe from exactly this kind of uncertainty.

The realm I just left taught me that emotions aren't weather that happens to you—they're tools you can learn to use consciously. But using them feels so dangerous. When I let myself really feel my regret about the choices I didn't make, the landscape showed me all the lives I might have lived. When I acknowledged my anger at myself for playing small, mountains literally moved. When I allowed myself to experience the full weight of missing you—yes, missing you, because you're becoming more real to me with every step of this journey—the very air around me shimmered with longing.

I saw the Prague job I turned down, Kit. I saw myself in that timeline, walking cobblestone streets and discovering manuscripts that would have changed everything about who I became. I saw the Seattle librarian I was too scared to have dinner with, and the love story that might have unfolded if I hadn't been so terrified of disappointment. I saw the writing group I didn't join, the Scotland trip I declined, the hundred small moments when I chose safety over possibility.

And it hurts. God, it hurts to see how different my life could have been if I'd just been braver.

It hurt, seeing all of that. But it also felt like waking up after years of sleepwalking through my own life.

The strangest part is how real you've become during this process. Not just theoretically real, but present somehow. I keep hearing echoes of your voice, keep finding myself thinking "Kit would love this" or "Kit would know what to do here." It's as if the more honest I become about my own feelings, the clearer the memory of you becomes.

Do you remember what you used to say about emotions? How most people were afraid of them because they confused feeling something with being overwhelmed by it? You said emotions were like weather systems—powerful and sometimes destructive, but also necessary for growth. You said the trick wasn't to avoid storms but to learn to dance in the rain.

I'm trying to learn that dance, Kit. I'm trying to let myself feel everything—the regret, the hope, the fear, the excitement about who I might become. But it's hard when you've spent decades trying to keep your emotional weather as calm and predictable as possible.

Sometimes I wonder if this is just an elaborate way of having a nervous breakdown. But if it is, it's the most educational breakdown in history.

The realm had a river that appeared whenever I felt sad about lost opportunities. At first I tried to stop being sad so the river would go away, but then I realized the river wasn't a problem to be solved. It was a feature of the landscape, as necessary as rainfall. When I stopped fighting it and just let myself grieve for the adventures I'd missed, something beautiful happened: the river became navigable. It didn't disappear, but it became something I could work with instead of something that worked against me.

I think you'd be proud of that realization. You always understood that the goal wasn't to avoid difficult feelings but to develop the skills to surf them.

I found an emotional mirror in that realm, Kit. It shows me the weather patterns of my own heart. Right now it's showing hope mixed with uncertainty, excitement tangled with fear, and underneath it all, a growing sense of recognition. As if I'm remembering not just who I used to be, but who I always was when I wasn't being careful about it.

I think you're real, Kit. Not just in the sense that you existed once, but real in the sense that you're still part of my story somehow. Every tool I'm learning to use, every insight I'm gaining—it all feels like remembering lessons you tried to teach me when we were young and I was too afraid to fully understand them.

If you're reading this somehow, if the magic of this place extends beyond its borders and finds its way to you, I want you to know: I'm finally learning to feel everything without being destroyed by it. I'm finally learning that courage isn't the absence of fear—it's fear transformed into fuel for growth.

Your emotionally awakening friend, Elsie

P.S. - The mirror showed me something else today: threads of connection stretching out from my heart like invisible strings. Most of them are tangled or broken, but one of them—the strongest one—stretches out toward something I can't quite see but somehow recognize. I think it leads to you. I think it always has.

CHAPTER 4
THE FEAST OF MEMORY

The air beyond the door tasted of August afternoons and forgotten birthday cakes, of promises whispered in tree houses and summer rain on hot pavement. It carried layers of scent that shouldn't have been able to coexist: library paste and honeysuckle, chalk dust and strawberry jam, playground swings and the drowsy warmth of afternoon naps on grandmother's quilts.

What the hell? Elsie's sinuses tingled like she was about to sneeze. The richness of it was overwhelming, as if her nose couldn't process so many memories layered into breathable air.

She stepped into what looked like an orchard, though the trees bore no earthly fruit. The ground felt soft and giving, like walking on centuries of fallen leaves. Each step released tiny puffs of scent—cinnamon and old books, grass stains and birthday candles—that rose around her ankles.

Instead of normal fruit, the branches hung heavy with translucent spheres that caught light like soap bubbles, each one glowing with different colors. Some pulsed with warm golden light that made her think of Christmas mornings, creating little pockets of heat she could feel against her skin. Others shimmered with silver melancholy that whispered of last days and made her shiver. A few flickered with deep purple of half-remembered dreams, their surfaces showing glimpses of faces that felt familiar but stayed just out of reach.

"Memory fruit," Minimus said softly, his voice unusually reverent. "Each one contains a moment someone chose to preserve. Not just facts, but the emotional essence, the meaning that made it worth remembering."

The trees seemed alive in a way that went beyond normal plants. Their bark had the warm texture of sun-heated skin, and when Elsie reached out experimentally, she could swear she felt a pulse beneath her palm. She could hear them humming—not audibly, but in her bones, a bass note so low it resonated in her chest.

The leaves rustled without wind, and she realized the trees were whispering to each other, voices like pages being turned in a distant library. The sound made her throat tighten with recognition, though she couldn't place why tree-conversation should feel familiar.

"How many memories are here?" she asked, looking around in wonder. The orchard stretched in every direction, disappearing into gentle golden haze.

"All of them," came a new voice, warm and melodious with the cadence of someone who'd told countless bedtime stories. The sound wrapped around Elsie like a favorite blanket.

A figure appeared from behind one of the trees. At first glance, she seemed like an elderly woman in a gardening apron, soil-stained and practical. But her hair was made of wisps of cloud that shifted color with her emotions—silver when serious, gold when pleased— and her skin had the translucent quality of moonlight on water. Her eyes held depths that suggested she'd witnessed countless memories across all of time.

"Welcome, dear one," the Feastkeeper said, her voice carrying warmth of grandmother's kitchen and mystery of starlight. The scent around her was complex—fresh bread and old roses, rain-washed earth and well-loved books. "I am Mira, tender of the

Memory Orchard. You arrive at an auspicious time—several fruits have been glowing brighter each time a certain name crosses your thoughts."

"Kit," Elsie said without thinking, and immediately felt warmth spread from her chest to her fingertips.

Mira smiled, and tiny flowers bloomed where her pleasure touched the air—delicate things that looked pressed from childhood diaries, petals translucent and glowing. The sight made Elsie's eyes water, though whether from beauty or something deeper, she couldn't say.

"Yes. That name has been causing quite a stir. The trees have been whispering about it for weeks, preparing fruit that's been waiting decades for the right person to taste."

Elsie looked around the orchard with new understanding, pulse quickening. "What exactly do the memory fruits do?"

"They help you remember," Mira said simply, reaching up to touch one of the glowing spheres. When her fingers made contact, the fruit chimed softly, and Elsie felt the note resonate in her sternum. "Not just facts or events, but the feeling-truth of moments that shaped you. Many travelers come here carrying memories they've forgotten, or feelings they've buried so deep they've convinced themselves those experiences were dreams."

She gestured to a nearby tree whose fruit glowed with warm amber. The air around it smelled of wood smoke and apple cider, crisp leaves and wool sweaters. "This tree grows memories of friendship—moments when souls recognize each other, when connections form that transcend ordinary social interaction."

Just being near the friendship tree made Elsie's chest ache with longing, throat tight with memory of connections she'd almost made, relationships she'd been too afraid to deepen. Her hands clenched involuntarily.

Another tree, its fruit shimmering silver-blue, caught her attention. The temperature around it was cooler, carrying the scent of libraries on rainy days.

"And that one?"

"Solitude," Mira said fondly, her cloud-hair shifting to gentle rose. "Not loneliness, but chosen aloneness—memories of moments when being by yourself felt like coming home. Reading by lamplight while storms rage outside, long walks where thoughts can unfurl, the satisfaction of your own company."

"What happens when you eat them?" Elsie asked, though part of her already knew from the way the fruit seemed to pulse with her heartbeat. Her mouth was watering despite herself.

"You experience the memory as if for the first time, but with the wisdom of who you've become since," Mira explained, leading her deeper into the grove. Her footsteps made no sound, but Elsie could feel the trees responding, branches rustling, fruit glowing brighter as they passed. "It can be... intense. Revelatory. Sometimes uncomfortable. But always necessary. Memories aren't just recordings—they're living things that continue to shape you. When you bury them or convince yourself they weren't real, they lose their power to teach and heal."

As they walked, Elsie found herself drawn to certain trees without understanding why. Her body seemed to recognize them before her mind did—a quickening pulse here, chest tightness there, hair standing up when she passed certain groves. One whose fruit glowed deep green seemed to call to her, spheres humming with whispered confidences and shared dreams.

Another tree, bearing fruit that shimmered like captured fireflies, made her think of magic felt but not understood, of childhood wonder that hadn't been educated away yet. As she passed beneath its branches, she could smell chalk dust and playground dirt, hear distant echo of children's laughter.

Minimus shifted on her shoulder, multifaceted eyes reflecting countless memory fruits like tiny kaleidoscopes. "I should mention that beetle memory works quite differently. We remember mostly in chemical signatures and navigational landmarks. Scent of danger, location of food sources, efficient paths between important places.

I'll be interested to observe how your species processes these more complex temporal emotional constructs."

His matter-of-fact tone was somehow comforting in this place where everything felt charged with emotional significance. The familiar weight of his small body kept her grounded even as the orchard's magic made her feel like she might float away.

Mira laughed, and the sound created tiny butterflies that fluttered between trees, each carrying fragments of joy to pollinate new memories. Where they landed, small flowers bloomed—living things that smelled like celebration and sounded like distant music in the breeze.

"Your companion is wise in his own way. Memory is different for each being. What matters isn't accuracy of what you remember, but the truth of what it teaches you about who you are and who you're becoming."

They paused beneath a tree whose fruit seemed to contain entire conversations—she could see tiny figures moving inside the translucent spheres, mouths moving in animated discussion. The fruit here radiated warmth like a fireplace, and the air smelled of coffee and old books, heated debates and the particular electricity of minds truly connecting.

"That one," Mira said softly, noticing where Elsie's gaze lingered, "has been waiting for you longer than any of the others."

The fruit was the color of deep forest shade shot through with gold, like sunlight filtering through leaves in a secret grove. It pulsed with warmth she could feel from several feet away, and whispered with voices too quiet to understand but too familiar to ignore. As she watched, vision blurring with unshed tears, she thought she glimpsed two figures inside—children, bent over a book, heads close together as they planned impossible adventures.

"Kit," she breathed, and the fruit grew brighter, warmth intensifying until she had to resist the urge to hold her hands up to it like a campfire.

"Memory fruit doesn't just preserve the past," Mira said gently, cloud-hair shifting to deep blue of sympathy. "It calls to those who need to understand something about their own story. This one has been glowing brighter each time you've thought about someone named Kit, each time you've wondered whether what you remember was real or just a beautiful dream your lonely heart created."

Elsie's chest tightened with something between hope and terror, hands shaking as she clasped them together. "What if I find out Kit was just wishful thinking? What if I made up this perfect friend because I needed someone who understood me?"

The possibility made her stomach clench. To discover that the most meaningful friendship of her childhood had been elaborate self-deception would retroactively hollow out every choice she'd made since.

"And what if you find out Kit was completely real?" Mira countered gently but challengingly. "What if the friendship that shaped your understanding of possibility and adventure was as true as sunrise? Which possibility frightens you more?"

The question hung in the air like a challenge, visible almost as a shimmering distortion. Elsie felt her knees lock involuntarily, her body's response to confronting truths she'd spent decades avoiding.

She thought about all the years she'd spent half-convinced that Kit existed only in childhood fantasy, a perfect friend conjured by a lonely girl's imagination. But also about the intensity of those memories, how they'd continued to influence her dreams even when she'd tried to dismiss them as fiction. Her palms were sweating now, and she wiped them nervously on her cardigan.

"I think," she said slowly, barely above a whisper, "I'm more afraid of finding out Kit was real."

"Why?"

"Because then I'd have to face how badly I failed them." The words rushed out, throat constricting. "How I broke every promise we made, how I chose safety over the adventures we planned, how I let fear make me small when I swore I would always dream big." Her voice caught, tears threatening. "If Kit was real, then I turned my back on someone who believed in me completely."

Mira reached up and plucked the memory fruit with careful reverence. It was warm and seemed to pulse with its own heartbeat, alive with possibilities. When she held it out, Elsie could feel its heat against her face, smell the scent rising from it—summer afternoons and library corners, ink stains and adventure plans, the particular sweetness of friendships that feel like coming home.

"What you're describing sounds like grief," Mira said gently, eyes holding depths of understanding. "Grief for the person you were before fear taught you to choose smaller dreams. But grief can be a doorway, not just an ending. Are you ready to remember what was true?"

Elsie looked at the fruit in Mira's weathered hands, feeling its warmth, watching it pulse like a living heart. Around them, the Memory Orchard hummed with collected experiences of countless lives, each fruit a testament to moments someone had decided were worth preserving. She thought about her journey so far—how she'd learned that size was about what you measured against, how emotions could be tools rather than weather, how every moment offered the choice between safety and growth.

Her hands were trembling now, but not just with fear. There was anticipation too, and deep, bone-level exhaustion with carrying uncertainty for so many years.

"What if it hurts?" she asked, voice small.

"Pain is often the price of truth," Mira said, cloud-hair shifting to silver. "But healing is usually the result. And you cannot heal what you refuse to remember."

Elsie accepted the memory fruit with both hands, marveling at its weight. Something so small shouldn't have felt so significant, but it seemed to contain entire worlds. The surface was warm and smooth, like sun-heated skin, and she could feel memories moving inside it like living things, eager to be released. Her pulse was racing now, mouth dry with anticipation.

"I need to know," she said, as much to herself as to Mira, voice growing steadier with resolution. "I need to know what was real."

She bit into the memory fruit.

The world dissolved into summer.

The taste exploded across her tongue—not just flavor, but experience itself, sweet and complex and so intensely nostalgic it made her chest ache. She was twelve again, sitting in the children's section on a drowsy afternoon when the air conditioning couldn't quite keep up with the heat. Dust motes danced in slanted sunlight that painted everything gold, and the library held that peculiar summer quiet where even turning pages seemed loud.

HER BODY REMEMBERED BEING TWELVE—THE way her legs didn't quite reach the floor in adult-sized chairs, how her summer tan made the pale skin under her watch band look like a negative photograph, the particular weight of her hair when it was long enough to braid but always escaping in wisps.

Across from her sat Kit—and suddenly Kit was completely, undeniably real: dark hair that never stayed neat despite constant attempts to smooth it down, eyes the color of creek water in spring shade, fingers always stained with ink from the fountain pen they insisted on using even though it made their handwriting blotchy. Kit wore a faded t-shirt with a compass rose and jean shorts with grass stains at the knees, and they smelled like adventure—like bicycle rides and tree climbing and the particular scent of someone who spent more time outdoors than most people considered proper.

The reality of Kit hit her like a physical blow—not imagined, not constructed from loneliness, but absolutely, completely real. She could see the small scar on Kit's chin from falling off their bike, could hear the way they breathed slightly through their mouth when concentrating, could smell the combination of soap and grass and something indefinably Kit that she had never been able to replicate or forget.

"When we grow up," Kit was saying, leaning across the small table where they'd spread fairy tale books like maps to unknown territories, voice pitched low so Mrs. Henderson wouldn't shush them, "we should become explorers. Real ones, not the kind that just climb mountains and plant flags and call it adventure."

"What kind of explorers would we be?" twelve-year-old Elsie asked, though she already knew Kit would have the answer planned out in elaborate detail. Kit always had plans, schemes, dreams mapped out with precision of military campaigns and ambition of someone who'd never learned that some things were impossible.

"The kind that find the places that exist in the spaces between things," Kit said, voice bright with certainty and warm with conviction that made even adults stop to listen. Their hands moved as they talked, sketching invisible maps in the air above open books, and Elsie could see every gesture with perfect clarity—the way Kit's thumb was double-jointed, the small callus on their middle finger from gripping pencils too tightly, the bitten-short nails always slightly dirty from adventures.

"We'd have a ship that sails on possibility instead of water, and we'd catalog wonders instead of just... ordinary stuff. We'd write guidebooks to places like the Valley of Lost Buttons and the City of Borrowed Time and the Mountains Where Music Goes to Sleep."

Kit's eyes were shining as they spoke, and Elsie could see herself reflected in them—not just her physical appearance, but Kit's vision of who she could become. In Kit's eyes, she was brave and clever and worthy of impossible adventures.

"That sounds impossible," Elsie had said, but her heart was racing with the beauty of it, twelve-year-old chest tight with the way Kit's certainty made even the most fantastical dreams feel achievable.

"The best things always do," Kit replied, reaching across to squeeze her hand. Their fingers were warm and ink-stained and completely solid, completely real. The pressure of Kit's grip was exactly as she remembered—firm but gentle, conveying absolute confidence and unshakeable friendship. "That's how you know they're worth finding. If something was easy, everyone would have done it already, and then it wouldn't be an adventure anymore."

The memory shimmered and shifted, carrying her forward with fluid dream logic. Suddenly they were fourteen, sitting by Miller's Creek during one of those endless summer evenings when the sky stayed light until almost nine and the world felt infinite with possibility. The air smelled of honeysuckle and creek water, and she could feel warm stone through her jeans, hear gentle sound of water moving over rocks.

Kit was reading aloud from a poetry book they'd discovered in a used bookstore, voice giving weight and music to words that spoke of journeys and transformations and courage required to become who you were meant to be. Their voice had started changing that summer, cracking occasionally in ways that embarrassed them but made Elsie feel protective and fond.

"Listen to this," Kit had said, finding a particular passage and reading with solemnity of someone sharing sacred text: "*'We are not nouns, we are verbs. I am not a thing... I am a person living a life.' Isn't that perfect? We're not fixed things—we're actions, stories in progress, adventures happening.*"

They closed the book and looked at her with unusual serious-ness, creek-water eyes reflecting the last light of day. In the memory, Elsie could see every detail of Kit's face—the way their eyebrows were slightly uneven, small freckles across their nose that only appeared in summer, the intensity that made their whole face seem to glow when they talked about things that mattered.

"Promise me something, Elsie. Promise me we won't forget how to dream big. Even when we get older and people tell us to be realis-tic, promise me we'll remember that being realistic just means you've given up on the interesting possibilities."

The weight of that promise sat heavy in fourteen-year-old Elsie's chest, serious and sacred in the way that only adolescent vows could be. She could feel the exact texture of the moment—cooling air against her skin, sound of insects beginning evening chorus, the way Kit's hand felt in hers, slightly sticky from heat but steady and sure.

"I promise," fourteen-year-old Elsie had said, meaning it with every fiber of her being, sealing the vow with intensity that only adolescents could bring to their most sacred commitments.

THE MEMORY SHIFTED AGAIN, more painfully now, and she was sixteen, standing in Kit's bedroom surrounded by packed boxes and terrible finality of change. Her body remembered the hollow ache in her chest, the way her throat kept closing up, the particular heaviness that came with goodbyes that felt too permanent to bear.

Kit's family was moving—Portland, that was it. Kit's mother had gotten a job at a university there, something about art history and a research position too good to pass up. The details felt sharp and clear now, no longer blurred by decades of trying to forget.

The room looked strange with Kit's belongings disappearing into cardboard containers. The maps they'd drawn together, carefully rolled up and secured with rubber bands. Books of poetry and fairy tales, wrapped in tissue paper like precious artifacts. The compass Kit's grandfather had given them, carefully nestled in a box marked "FRAGILE" in Kit's distinctive handwriting—all loops and flourishes that somehow managed to be both elegant and completely readable.

"It's not forever," Kit had said, but their voice carried doubt for the first time since Elsie had known them. They were trying to be brave, but she could see the fear underneath—sixteen years old and being forced to leave behind everything familiar, everyone who knew them and loved them exactly as they were.

They pressed a small notebook into Elsie's hands—leather-bound, with pages so soft they felt like fabric. The cover was embossed with a compass rose identical to the one on Kit's favorite t-shirt. The leather was warm from Kit's hands, and it smelled like the art supplies Kit was always carrying around—pencils and erasers and the particular scent of creativity.

"This is for you to write back," Kit said, voice urgent with need to make her understand how important this was. "All your adventures, all your discoveries. Millbrook has mysteries too, I bet. Hidden places we never found, stories we never uncovered. You can be an explorer right here while I'm being one out there, and we'll share everything through letters."

Kit's hands were shaking slightly as they spoke, and Elsie realized with shock that her perfectly confident friend was just as terrified as she was. Maybe more so, because Kit was the one who had to leave everything familiar and venture into unknown territory without any guarantee they'd find their place in a new world.

"Promise me," Kit said, voice breaking slightly on the words, "promise me you'll write. Promise me you'll keep exploring, keep looking for the magical places and the impossible things. Promise me that when you're ready for that big adventure we always talked about, you'll know how to find me. Real explorers always know how to find each other."

The weight of Kit's hands on hers, the intensity in their eyes, the smell of their room (art supplies and summer air and the indefinable scent that was just Kit)—everything was so clear, so undeniably real that it made her current self weep with the certainty of it.

"I promise," sixteen-year-old Elsie had said, clutching the notebook like a lifeline, meaning it just as completely as she had meant every other promise she'd ever made to Kit. "I promise I'll write, and I'll explore, and I'll find you when it's time."

But she hadn't written. The memory showed her that truth too, equally clear and painful: the notebook sitting on her desk for weeks, then months, then migrating to a drawer as guilt and time made writing feel more impossible. At first she'd been too heartbroken, then too embarrassed by how long she'd waited, then too convinced that Kit had moved on to new friends and new dreams that didn't include a small-town librarian who had never learned to be brave.

The memory fruit's magic released her gently, returning her to the present with the taste of truth on her tongue and weight of understanding in her heart. She was forty-five again, standing in an impossible orchard, but Kit's reality blazed through her like sunlight, undeniable and transformative.

"Kit was real," she said wonderingly, tears streaming down her cheeks without shame. Her whole body was shaking with the magnitude of it, with relief and grief and joy all tangled together. "They were completely, absolutely real."

"Yes," Mira said simply, settling beside her on soft grass beneath the memory tree. The Feastkeeper's presence was warm and solid, anchoring her to the present while she processed the overwhelming return of truth. "And what else?"

Elsie thought about the promises they'd made, the dreams they'd shared, the explorer's life they'd planned together with such certainty and joy. She thought about the safe, small life she'd built instead, and how every careful choice had been, in its way, a betrayal of that sixteen-year-old who had sworn not to forget how to dream big.

Her throat constricted as she spoke the truth aloud: "I broke my promise. I forgot how to dream big. I chose safety over possibility so many times that I forgot possibility even existed. I let fear teach me to play small when I'd sworn to always think large."

The words tasted bitter, but also somehow cleansing—like medicine that hurt going down but began healing immediately.

"And what would Kit say about that?" Mira asked gently.

Elsie closed her eyes and let herself imagine it—Kit at forty-five, probably ink-stained still, probably still believing in the impossible with that same unshakeable conviction that had made them magnetic as children. She could almost see them: wearing practical clothes that somehow looked adventurous, carrying a notebook full of sketches and observations, eyes bright with accumulated wisdom of someone who had spent their life seeking out the magical and mysterious.

Kit would look at her with those creek-water eyes and say something like: *So you took a detour through Safety Land. So what? The best explorers are always getting lost and finding better paths than the ones they originally planned. The question isn't whether you've been living the dream we shared—it's whether you're ready to start living it now.*

The imagined words felt so real, so completely in Kit's voice, that for a moment she could swear she heard them spoken aloud. Her spine straightened with something that felt like hope mixed with determination.

"They'd say it's not too late," she said aloud, opening her eyes to find Mira watching her with approval that made her cloud-hair shift to golden contentment.

"Is it?" Mira asked.

Elsie looked around the Memory Orchard, with its constellation of preserved moments and testament to the truth that what we remember shapes who we become. She thought about the atlas that had started her journey—not the physical book anymore, but the sense of possibility it had awakened. She thought about the realms she'd already traveled, the parts of herself she'd reclaimed, the tools she'd learned to use: understanding that scale was about what you measured against, knowing that emotions were information rather than weather, accepting that courage was a choice available in every moment.

She thought about the emotional mirror in her pocket, warm against her hip, showing her the complex weather of a heart learning to be honest. She could feel its gentle pulse even now, reflecting back the mixture of grief and hope and determination that was currently painting her emotional landscape in colors that had no names but felt like sunrise.

"No," she said, and the word rang with the same certainty that had once lived in Kit's voice, resonating in her chest like a bell being struck. "It's not too late. It's never too late to become who you were meant to be."

Mira smiled, and where her joy touched the ground, new memory trees began to sprout—saplings whose fruit glowed not with preserved past moments, but with shimmer of experiences yet to be lived, adventures yet to be undertaken, stories yet to be written. The sight made Elsie's breath catch with wonder and possibility.

"Then you're ready for this," the Feastkeeper said, reaching into her apron and withdrawing what looked like a seed but glowed with its own inner light. The light was warm and golden, like concentrated sunlight, and just looking at it made Elsie feel more alive, more present, more ready for whatever came next.

"This will grow into memories you haven't made yet, but which are already taking root in the soil of your intention. Plant it when you're ready to start living the adventures you've been dreaming."

Elsie accepted the seed with reverence, feeling its potential pulse warm against her palm like a tiny heartbeat. The warmth spread up her arm and settled in her chest, a physical reminder of possibilities waiting to be claimed.

"Thank you. For the fruit, for the truth, for helping me remember." Her voice was steady now, stronger than it had been since entering the orchard.

"Thank the trees," Mira said, gesturing to the memory grove around them. "And thank yourself for having courage to taste what you'd buried. Many travelers pass through this orchard without accepting even a single fruit. They're too afraid of what they might discover about their own stories."

As if in response to her gratitude, the orchard around them began to shift and change, revealing paths she hadn't noticed before. Some led deeper into the grove, where she could see other travelers moving among trees, some laughing with joy at recovered memories, others weeping with beauty of what they'd thought was lost forever. But her attention was drawn to a familiar sight: another doorway, this one carved from what looked like crystallized ink and bound with shadows that seemed to move independently of any light source.

The sight of it made her stomach clench with recognition and anticipation. She could smell something emanating from beyond the door—the scent of old paper and forgotten stories, but also something darker, more complex. The smell of things deliberately erased, of stories that had been written out of existence.

Above the door, words appeared in elegant script, though these seemed to write themselves more slowly, as if reluctant to be seen: *The Archive of Inkless Names.*

"A shadowy archive that collects erased stories," she read aloud, remembering the description from the atlas. A chill ran through her that had nothing to do with temperature and everything to do with recognition. Her skin prickled with goosebumps, her body recognizing danger even when her mind was ready for the challenge. "The parts of myself that I've been editing away."

Minimus shifted uneasily on her shoulder, tiny claws gripping her cardigan with more tension than she'd felt from him before. "That's where the real test begins. Are you ready to face the stories that were written out of existence? The versions of yourself that you decided weren't worth keeping?"

Elsie looked at the memory seed in her palm, then at the door that promised confrontation with everything she'd tried to forget or deny about herself. She thought of Kit's voice saying *Real explorers always know how to find each other*, and realized that perhaps the person she most needed to find was the version of herself she'd lost along the way—not just the dreaming child, but all the discarded possibilities, the abandoned selves, the stories she'd erased because they felt too risky or impractical or strange.

The seed pulsed warmer in her palm, as if responding to her resolution. She tucked it carefully into her pocket beside Sym's emotional mirror, feeling the weight of tools and truth she'd gathered on this journey.

"Yes," she said, voice steady despite the way her heart was

hammering against her ribs. "I think I'm ready to meet all the versions of myself I've been hiding from."

"Good," said a voice that was not Mira's, not Minimus's, and not quite her own—though it carried echoes of her voice as it might have been if she'd made different choices, taken different risks, chosen growth over safety at crucial moments. The voice seemed to come from the direction of the Archive, carrying with it the weight of stories untold and selves unchosen.

Elsie turned toward the voice, skin tingling with awareness, but saw only shadows shifting at the edges of the orchard, and the distant gleam of eyes that reflected library light and held accumulated weight of every story she'd ever refused to write, every adventure she'd ever declined, every version of herself she'd ever decided wasn't worth becoming.

The door to the Archive stood open, breathing the scent of old paper and forgotten stories into the sweet air of the Memory Orchard. Whatever waited beyond—her shadow self, her discarded possibilities, the confrontation with everything she'd spent decades avoiding—Elsie knew it would require all the tools she'd gathered. The understanding of scale. An ability to work with emotions. Courage to face the full truth of her own story. And now, the knowledge that some promises, even when broken, could still be kept if you had enough honesty and hope.

She stepped toward the doorway, carrying with her the taste of summer afternoons and knowledge that Kit had been real, that their friendship had been the truest thing in her childhood, and that the dreams they'd shared were still waiting patiently for her to claim them.

Behind her, Mira tended to her impossible trees, humming a tune that sounded like lullabies and adventure songs and the music that plays when someone finally remembers who they used to be and decides to become that person again, older and wiser but no less willing to believe in the magical and impossible.

INTERLUDE #3: LETTER TO KIT

Written on paper that seems to hold the faint scent of summer afternoons and has the soft texture of memory itself

My dearest Kit,

I know you're real now. Not because of logic or evidence, but because I've tasted the truth of you in a way that goes deeper than mere knowledge. I've been to a place where memories grow like fruit on impossible trees, and I bit into the green sphere that contained us at twelve, planning adventures we were certain we'd live together.

Jesus. I actually wrote that sentence and meant it. Six months ago I would have committed myself for thinking thoughts like that.

Do you remember that afternoon in the library? The summer heat making everything drowsy and golden, dust motes dancing in the slanted light while we spread fairy tale books across the table like maps to unknown countries? You were so certain about our future as explorers—not the kind who just climb mountains and plant flags, but the kind who would find the places that exist in the spaces between things.

You said we'd have a ship that sails on possibility instead of water. You said we'd catalog wonders instead of just ordinary stuff. The way you spoke about it, with such complete conviction that even impossible things seemed not just possible but inevitable—I can still feel the way that certainty lit up something inside me, the way it made me believe I was someone capable of extraordinary things.

I tasted that belief again today, Kit. After decades of thinking I'd imagined it, I experienced it as clearly as if no time had passed at all. The way you looked at me when you talked about our plans—not like I was someone you were trying to convince, but like I was someone who already understood, who was already your partner in whatever adventure came next.

Do you remember the promises we made? By Miller's Creek that evening when the sky stayed light forever and you read poetry aloud until the words became part of the air itself? You made me swear we wouldn't forget how to dream big, wouldn't let anyone convince us to be realistic when realistic just meant giving up on the interesting possibilities.

I broke that promise, Kit. I'm not telling you this for forgiveness—I'm telling you because the memory fruit showed me something else: that you would understand. That you would look at me with those creek-water eyes and say something like, "So you took a detour. So what? The best explorers always get lost before they find the really interesting places."

But I wonder if that's just what I want you to say. If I'm creating a version of you that tells me what I need to hear.

But I wonder: do you remember these moments the same way I do? When you think back to those summer afternoons and endless evening conversations, do you see the same scenes that played out in perfect detail when I bit into that impossible fruit? Or do memories work differently for the person who stayed brave, who kept exploring, who never let fear teach them to choose smaller dreams?

I've been thinking about the notebook you gave me when you moved away. The leather-bound one with the compass rose that was supposed to hold all my adventures while you were discovering new ones in Portland. I still have it, Kit. It's been sitting in a drawer for decades, blank pages waiting patiently for someone brave enough to fill them with stories worth telling.

I think I'm almost ready to write in it again. Not to record the adventure I'm having now—this journey through impossible realms—but to begin the adventures I want to have when I return to the ordinary world. Because I understand now that the magic isn't just in the places you can only reach through enchanted atlases. The magic is in choosing to live fully enough that your regular life becomes an adventure worth documenting.

The memory fruit showed me something beautiful, Kit: even in the moments when I was disappointing you by choosing safety over possibility, you never stopped believing in the version of me that was brave enough to explore the impossible. That belief lived in you like a seed, waiting for the right conditions to sprout into something I could recognize and reclaim.

I'm reclaiming it now. Slowly, carefully, but with growing confidence. Each realm I visit teaches me something about the person I was before I learned to be afraid, and about the person I'm still capable of becoming.

There's another door waiting for me, another realm to explore. But for the first time since this journey began, I'm not afraid of what I might find there. Because I know now that whatever I discover will be something you always knew was inside me, waiting for me to be brave enough to look.

With all my love and remembering, Elsie

P.S. - The Feastkeeper gave me a seed today. She said it would grow into memories I haven't made yet, experiences that are already taking root in the soil of my intentions. I'm carrying it with me, this promise of adventures still to come. I think you'd like that—the idea that the future can be as real as the past if you're willing to believe in it strongly enough.

CHAPTER 5

THE ARCHIVE OF INKLESS NAMES

The first thing Elsie noticed about the Archive was the silence—not the comfortable, breathing quiet of a library at rest, but the oppressive hush of a place where words had been systematically removed. It pressed against her eardrums like deep water, making her hyperaware of her own heartbeat, her own breathing, the soft scratch of Minimus's tiny claws adjusting their grip on her shoulder.

Something's wrong here. Her mouth was already going dry.

The second thing she noticed was the cold. Not winter cold, but the chill of abandonment, of things left untended and unloved. Her breath misted as she stepped through the doorway, and she pulled her cardigan closer, though she suspected the cold came from more than temperature. The fabric felt thin against her skin, useless against whatever waited in this place.

The Archive stretched before her in impossible dimensions, its ceiling lost in shadows that seemed to move independently. Endless rows of shelves rose into darkness, but instead of books, they held empty spaces—not vacant shelves, but carefully maintained voids where books should have been, each absence outlined in faint silver lines. The air itself felt hollow, carved away.

Who builds a library for things that don't exist? Her throat was getting tighter.

"The stories that were never allowed to exist," Minimus whispered, barely audible in the oppressive quiet. "The narratives that someone—often the author herself—decided weren't worth keeping."

As her eyes adjusted to the strange half-light that seemed to come from the empty spaces themselves, Elsie began to make out figures moving between the shelves. Translucent, ghostlike beings made of pale ink and fading paper. They moved with librarian purposefulness, cataloging and organizing, but their efforts made no sound—no footsteps, no rustle of paper, no whispered consultations.

They're tending to nothing, she realized, watching one of the beings carefully dust an empty space with a cloth that left no trace. *Just like—*

The thought stopped as fear crystallized in her chest.

"The Inkless," came a voice from deeper in the Archive, and Elsie felt a chill that had nothing to do with temperature. The sound cut through the quiet like a blade, sharp and familiar and wrong. "They tend to the spaces where stories used to be. They remember what was erased, though they can no longer speak it aloud."

Elsie's hands began to tremble. She knew that voice—it was her own, but drained of warmth, sharpened by years of disappointment. Her mouth went dry as understanding flooded through her, cold and inevitable.

The speaker approached, and Elsie understood with sick certainty why the voice was so familiar. It was herself, but a version carved away by disappointment and fear. This other Elsie wore the same face, but pinched with perpetual dissatisfaction, marked by lines of criticism and self-denial. Her hair was pulled back so severely it seemed to cause pain, and her clothes—the same cardigan and sensible skirt—looked somehow smaller, more restrictive, as if they'd been tailored to constrain rather than comfort.

She looks like me if I'd never laughed. Never hoped. Never allowed myself a single moment of joy.

"So," the shadow librarian said, voice carrying decades of accumulated resentment, "you finally decided to visit. How convenient. How typically late."

"Who are you?" Elsie asked, though she already knew the answer would be complicated and unwelcome. The words came out smaller than she'd intended, shrinking in the Archive's consuming silence.

"I'm the part of you that kept you safe," the shadow replied, moving closer with predatory grace perfected over years of cutting observations. "I'm the voice that reminded you that dreams are for children, that practical choices lead to stable lives, that disappointment is the inevitable result of hoping for too much."

She gestured to the Archive around them, movements precise and economical in the way of someone who'd learned to take up as little space as possible. The gesture stirred the air, and Elsie caught the scent of old paper and abandoned ink—the smell of stories that had died before they could be told.

"I'm the part of you that edited out all the messy, impractical, embarrassing bits. The part that decided some stories weren't worth keeping."

As she spoke, the empty spaces on the shelves began to shimmer, and Elsie caught glimpses of what had been erased. Books that flickered in and out of existence: *The Adventures of Elsie and Kit* by E. Vine, *Letters from Prague: A Librarian's European Journey* by Elsie Vine, *Love Songs from Seattle: A Collection* by E.V. Poetry collections never written, travel memoirs never lived, love stories never allowed to begin.

All those stories. All those versions of myself I never allowed to exist.

The sight hit her like a physical blow. Her chest ached with the weight of recognition—not just of the lost stories, but of the part of herself that had systematically destroyed them.

"I saved you from embarrassment," the shadow librarian contin-ued, defending a long-held position. "From failure. From the pain of trying and not measuring up. From the humiliation of caring too much about things that don't matter to practical people."

But caring about things is what makes life worth living, Elsie real-ized, the thought arising with startling clarity. *The humiliation of caring too much is better than the emptiness of caring too little.*

"You saved me from living," Elsie said quietly.

The shadow's face twisted with anger, and the temperature seemed to drop another degree. Frost began to form on the empty shelves, outlining the absent stories in crystalline detail. "I saved you from suffering! Do you know what would have happened if you'd gone to Prague? You would have been mediocre. A small-town librarian pretending to understand medieval manuscripts, embar-rassing yourself in front of real scholars. Do you know what would have happened if you'd pursued that man in Seattle? He would have discovered that you're not as interesting as you seemed at a confer-ence, and you would have been discarded like last week's newspaper."

With each harsh prediction, books flickered more violently on the shelves—not just the ones that had been erased, but the ones that might still be written. The empty spaces pulsed like wounds, and Elsie watched volumes appear and disappear: *The Cartographer's Compass: A Guide to Emotional Territories, Finding Kit: A Story of Lost and Found Friendship, The Atlas of Second Chances.*

The sight of that last title made something fierce and protective rise in her chest. *Those stories want to exist. They're not gone—they're imprisoned. And I'm the one who locked them away.*

"You don't know that," Elsie said, finding unexpected strength in her voice. Her words seemed to push back against the Archive's oppressive silence, creating small pockets of warmth. "You don't know what would have happened because you never let me try."

"I know because I understand reality," the shadow snapped, and now the Inkless beings moved more frantically, translucent forms flickering as the Archive responded to emotional turbulence. Some of the empty spaces began to leak—not ink, but something that looked like liquid disappointment, flowing down the shelves and pooling on the floor with the sound of tears falling on paper.

"I understand limitations. I understand that some people are meant for ordinary lives, and there's nothing wrong with accepting that. The problem isn't that you dreamed small—it's that you dreamed at all."

But dreams are maps. They show you where you might go, not where you must go. And even if you never reach them, they teach you something about the territory of your own heart.

The Archive pulsed with the shadow's anger, and the sounds of distress grew louder—whispered sobs of stories that had never been allowed to draw breath, the rustle of pages that existed only in potential, the soft thud of books falling from shelves that existed only in memory.

"Look around you," the shadow continued, gesturing to endless shelves of absence. "Look at all the stories I prevented you from writing badly. All the humiliation I saved you from experiencing. All the pain I helped you avoid. Isn't a safe, predictable life better than a chaotic, unsuccessful one?"

Elsie looked around the Archive, really seeing it for the first time. The careful maintenance of emptiness, the Inkless beings preserving nothing with such dedication, the cold silence where there should have been the warm buzz of stories being shared and treasured. She thought of Mira's Memory Orchard, where even failed dreams bore fruit that could nourish future growth.

This place is the opposite of that orchard. This is what happens when you're so afraid of failure that you refuse to plant anything at all.

"No," she said, and her voice carried the authority of someone who had learned to read the language of her own heart. The word seemed to create ripples in the Archive's oppressive atmosphere, and several of the Inkless beings paused in their futile cataloging to look toward her. "A safe, predictable life isn't better if it isn't really lived."

She reached into her pocket and withdrew Sym's emotional mirror, fingers warm against its surface. She held it up so both she and her shadow could see what it reflected. The image showed two emotional patterns: her own, swirling with colors of hope and fear and determination and grief, complex and contradictory and vibrantly alive; and the shadow's, a tight knot of grey and brown, controlled and contained and almost entirely lifeless.

"Look at us," Elsie said, heart racing with the courage of finally speaking truth. "Look at what your version of safety has cost. You've preserved me like a specimen in a jar—technically intact, but not actually living."

The shadow librarian stared at the mirror, and for the first time, something like uncertainty flickered across her face. When she spoke, her voice had lost some of its sharp certainty. "I was protecting you."

She was. She really believed she was saving me from pain. But she saved me right out of my own life.

"You were protecting an idea of me," Elsie corrected gently, the words emerging from understanding rather than anger. "A version of me that was so afraid of being hurt that she forgot how to be happy. A version that was so worried about failing that she never tried to succeed."

Around them, the Archive began to change. The oppressive silence lifted slightly, replaced by something that sounded almost like held breath—as if the space itself was waiting to see what would happen next. Some of the Inkless beings paused in their futile cataloging to look toward their conversation, and the empty spaces on the shelves shimmered more steadily, stories struggling to rematerialize like flowers pushing through snow.

"But what if you try and fail?" the shadow asked, and now her voice held something that sounded almost like pleading. The harsh lines of her face seemed to soften slightly, and Elsie could see the fear beneath the criticism—not malice, but terror of a pain so deep it had driven her to choose numbness over feeling. "What if you write that book and no one reads it? What if you reach out to Kit and they don't remember you, or don't care? What if you take risks and they don't pay off?"

Elsie thought about the journey that had brought her here—learning that size was about what you measured against; discovering that feelings were tools rather than weather; recovering the truth about Kit and the promises they'd made. Each realm had taught her something about the difference between existing and living, between safety and growth.

Failure is also a story. Even disappointment teaches you about the shape of your hopes.

"Then at least I'll have tried," she said, voice growing stronger with each word. "At least I'll have stories to tell, even if they're stories about failure. At least I'll have lived fully enough to have something worth remembering."

She pulled the memory seed from her pocket, the one Mira had given her that contained potential for experiences yet to be lived. It glowed warmly in the cold Archive, its light causing some of the nearest empty spaces to flicker with possibility. The warmth seemed to spread through her fingers, up her arms, settling in her chest like a small sun.

"I'm not saying there's no place for caution," she continued, speaking as much to herself as to the shadow. "I'm not saying every dream should be pursued without thought or preparation. But you went too far. You erased so much of me that I almost forgot I existed."

The shadow librarian looked around the Archive, perhaps seeing it clearly for the first time. The endless rows of carefully maintained absences, the Inkless beings preserving emptiness, the cold silence where there should have been warm buzz of stories being told and retold and transformed in the telling. Her reflection in Sym's mirror showed the tight knot of emotion beginning to loosen, threads of color bleeding through the grey.

"I thought I was keeping you safe," she said quietly, and now she sounded less like a harsh critic and more like a frightened child.

She was frightened. All this time, she wasn't trying to hurt me—she was trying to save me from a world that seemed too dangerous to navigate. She became cruel because she was terrified.

"I know," Elsie said, voice gentle with newfound compassion. "And some of that was necessary. Some of that probably saved me from real harm. But safety isn't supposed to be the only goal. Safety is supposed to be the foundation you build adventures on, not the walls you hide behind."

One of the Inkless beings approached them, translucent form shimmering with what might have been hope. The sound of its movement was like pages whispering against each other, soft and musical after the oppressive silence. It pointed to one of the empty spaces on the nearest shelf, and as Elsie watched, words began to appear in faint silver letters: *The Atlas of Elsewhere: A Journey Through the Geography of the Heart* by Elsie Vine.

"Oh," Elsie breathed, understanding flooding through her like warm honey. The title pulsed with its own inner light, and she could almost feel the weight of the book it wanted to become—not heavy, but substantial, real, important. "The stories aren't gone. They're just waiting for permission to exist."

The shadow librarian stared at the appearing title, her face cycling through expressions of fear, longing, and something that might have been pride. The harsh lines around her eyes were softening, and her posture was becoming less rigid, as if invisible bindings were loosening. "You would really write about this? About talking beetles and emotion smiths and memory fruit? People would think you were crazy."

Let them. Let them think I'm wonderfully, beautifully, completely mad. At least they'll think I'm something.

"Maybe," Elsie said, feeling lighter than she had in years. "But maybe some people would think it was wonderful. Maybe some people need to know that there are doorways hidden in ordinary libraries, that maps exist for territories of the heart, that it's never too late to become an explorer of the impossible."

More titles were appearing on the shelves now, as if the possibility of one story existing had given permission for others. Some were books she might write, others were experiences she might live, still others were versions of herself she might become. The Archive was transforming from a monument to absence into a catalog of potential, and the air itself seemed to grow warmer, more breathable.

Kit's Guide to Emotional Cartography, appeared on one shelf, the title glowing with warmth and humor. *Letters to My Younger Self: A Librarian's Manifesto. The Courage to Begin Again: Stories of Second Chances.*

Each new title felt like a door opening, like a hand extended in invitation, like a promise she was finally ready to make to herself.

"What happens to me?" the shadow asked, and there was something almost childlike in the question. The transformation was accelerating now—her severe hairstyle was relaxing into something softer, her constricting clothes were becoming more comfortable, and her voice was warming toward something recognizably Elsie's own. "If you start taking risks, if you stop letting fear make your decisions, what happens to the part of you that kept you safe?"

Elsie considered this, watching as more stories flickered into potential existence around them. The Archive was filling with light and warmth, the Inkless beings were gaining color and substance, and she could hear the beginning of what sounded like quiet conversations—stories talking to each other, sharing wisdom and hope.

She doesn't have to disappear. She just has to learn a new job.

"You become what you were always supposed to be," she said finally, the understanding settling in her chest like a key finding its lock. "Not the voice that says no to everything, but the voice that helps me choose wisely. Not the part that prevents all risk, but the part that helps me take intelligent risks."

She reached out her hand to the shadow librarian, palm up,

offering connection rather than demanding it. "I need you. Just not as the editor of my entire life. I need you as a counselor, a consultant. Someone who helps me think through consequences without preventing me from acting entirely."

The shadow looked at the offered hand with something that might have been longing. Her transformation was nearly complete now—she looked like Elsie still, but a version who had learned to be kind to herself, who wore wisdom instead of criticism, who had found the courage to be gentle.

"And if I can't change? If I'm too used to being the voice that says no?"

She's afraid too. Afraid of becoming something new, afraid of not being needed, afraid of failing in a different way. We're both scared of the same thing—the risk of being insufficient.

"Then we'll practice," Elsie said simply, voice warm with promise. "Like learning any new skill. You can learn to say 'be careful' instead of 'don't try,' 'think it through' instead of 'it's impossible,' 'proceed with wisdom' instead of 'give up before you start.'"

Slowly, hesitantly, the shadow reached out and took Elsie's hand. Her fingers were warm—not cold like the Archive, but alive with possibility. The moment their fingers touched, something extraordinary happened.

The transformation of the Archive accelerated dramatically. The cold lifted completely, replaced by the comfortable warmth of a well-loved library. The oppressive silence gave way to gentle hum of stories sharing themselves with each other—not loud, but alive, like the murmur of bees in a garden or the rustle of leaves in gentle breeze.

The shadow librarian's appearance completed its transformation. She looked like Elsie still, but a version who had learned that kindness to oneself was not weakness but strength, that wisdom could be gentle, that protection could nurture rather than constrain.

"I think," the shadow said, her voice now warm and recognizably Elsie's own—not a harsh critic but a trusted friend, "I might be willing to try being the voice of wise caution instead of paralyzing fear."

Around them, the final transformation of the Archive unfolded like flowers blooming in fast-forward. Empty spaces filled with books that glowed with their own inner light, each one representing not just a story that might be written, but a life that might be lived, a choice that might be made with both courage and wisdom. The former Inkless beings gained full substance and color as they found actual stories to tend, their translucent forms becoming solid librarians who moved with purpose and joy.

But not everything changed, and Elsie found herself grateful for that. Some empty spaces remained, and she realized these represented stories that truly weren't worth pursuing—genuine mistakes, harmful choices, paths that would have led to real damage rather than mere embarrassment. The shadow had been right about some things, and those lessons were worth keeping.

Wisdom isn't about saying yes to everything. It's about learning to tell the difference between risks worth taking and dangers worth avoiding. And I couldn't learn that difference alone—I needed both parts of myself.

"Remarkable integration," Minimus observed from her shoulder, voice carrying scientific interest rather than emotional investment. "I've never seen a consciousness successfully negotiate with its own shadow aspect before. Most species simply suppress or are overwhelmed by such confrontations."

One of the newly substantial former-Inkless beings approached them, and Elsie was surprised to see that it looked like a librarian— not ghostly anymore, but solid and warm, wearing clothes that somehow managed to look both professional and adventurous. The being's footsteps made soft, real sounds on the floor, and its smile was warm enough to chase away the last echoes of the Archive's former coldness.

"Thank you," the being said, voice carrying the musical quality of someone who spent their time surrounded by stories that were loved and shared. "We've been waiting so long for someone to give the erased stories permission to exist again. The Archive has been rather depressing without anything to actually archive."

They were waiting for me to forgive myself. Waiting for me to stop punishing myself for dreams I'd abandoned, for choices I'd been too afraid to make.

"What happens now?" Elsie asked, looking around at the transformed space that was rapidly becoming a real library rather than a monument to absence. Books hummed softly on their shelves, and she could see comfortable reading chairs appearing in sunny alcoves, cozy spots where visitors might sit and discover which stories called to them.

"Now you choose," the being said, gesturing toward a doorway that was materializing at the far end of the Archive. Unlike the doors she'd passed through before, this one looked familiar—it had the warm wood and brass fittings of the Millbrook Public Library, but somehow the familiar seemed touched by magic now, as if ordinary things had remembered they could be doorways to extraordinary places.

"You can return to your regular life, carrying with you everything you've learned, or you can continue deeper into the realms. There are always more territories to explore, more aspects of yourself to discover and integrate."

Elsie looked at the familiar doorway, then at her shadow self, who now stood beside her as an advisor rather than an opponent. She felt the memory seed warm in her pocket, felt Sym's mirror reflecting back an emotional pattern that was complex but no longer fractured, felt Minimus's small weight on her shoulder—not a burden but a reminder that wisdom could be found in the most unexpected places.

She thought about her journey so far, about the tools she'd gathered and the parts of herself she'd reclaimed. She thought about Kit, somewhere in Portland, probably still ink-stained and still believing in impossible adventures, still waiting for a letter that might bridge the years between what was and what could be.

I have work to do. Stories to plant, connections to rebuild, a life to begin living instead of just enduring.

"I think," she said, pulling out the memory seed that Mira had given her, watching it pulse with warm light in the transformed Archive, "I'm ready to start planting some new stories. But first, I have a letter to write."

The shadow librarian smiled—the first genuine smile Elsie had seen from her, warm and encouraging and full of possibility. "That sounds like a very reasonable place to start."

Together, they walked toward the door that would take them home, but home to a library that would never look quite the same to someone who knew that books could be doorways, that stories could reshape reality, and that the most important maps were the ones that led not to places, but to the unexplored territories of the self.

Behind them, the Archive hummed with new life, its shelves filling with stories that were finally allowed to exist, its librarians— no longer Inkless—caring for tales that were both cautionary and inspiring, teaching visitors the difference between wise caution and paralyzing fear.

In one of the reading alcoves that had appeared with the Archive's transformation, a small sign materialized, written in elegant script: *"Here are kept the stories that someone decided were worth risking, worth attempting, worth living—even when the outcome was uncertain. These are the chronicles of those who chose growth over safety, adventure over comfort, the possible over the merely practical."*

And below that, in smaller text: *"Failure is also a story worth keeping, if it comes from the attempt to live fully."*

The door to home stood open, warm and welcoming, but Elsie knew that home would now be not just the end of a journey, but the beginning of countless others. The atlas had taught her that maps were tools for exploration, not just navigation—and she was finally ready to explore not just the impossible realms beyond library doors, but the infinite possibilities that existed within a life consciously chosen rather than accidentally lived.

INTERLUDE #4: LETTER TO KIT

Written on paper that seems to shimmer between the stationery of the Millbrook Public Library and something that might have been torn from the Archive of Inkless Names

Dear Kit,

I almost didn't write this letter. I sat here for twenty minutes, pen in hand, telling myself all the reasons why I shouldn't: you might not remember me, you might not want to hear from me after all these years of silence, you might think I've lost my mind entirely when you read what I have to tell you.

You might think I've lost my mind because I probably have.

But then I realized that the voice listing those reasons was the same one that's been editing my life for decades, cutting out all the risky, messy, potentially wonderful parts. And I just spent what feels like a lifetime learning that some stories are worth the risk of being misunderstood.

So here's the truth, Kit. All of it, strange as it sounds.

You were real. I know that seems like an odd thing to say

—of course you were real—but I've spent so many years convincing myself that you might have been just a beautiful dream my lonely childhood heart created. The perfect friend who understood my hunger for impossible adventures, who saw magic in the ordinary world, who made me promise never to stop dreaming big. It seemed too good to be true, so I let myself believe it wasn't true at all.

Because if you were real, that meant I really did fail you. That meant my cowardice had real consequences for a real person.

But it was. You were real, and our friendship was real, and those promises we made under the summer sky were real. I know because I've been on the kind of adventure we used to plan together, the kind we swore we'd take when we were old enough and brave enough and ready for the impossible.

I found a book, Kit. An atlas that shouldn't exist, filled with maps to places that can't be real but somehow are. I've walked through realms where thoughts become geography, where emotions reshape the very ground beneath your feet, where memories grow on trees like fruit waiting to be tasted. I've learned that courage isn't the absence of fear—it's the willingness to let fear be information rather than a prison. I've discovered that the voice in my head that always said "be practical, be safe, don't risk disappointment" wasn't wisdom —it was just one possibility among many, and not even the best one.

I've remembered who I was before I learned to be afraid of being hurt. Do you remember that girl? The one who believed in secret doors and hidden countries and the possibility that the world was far more magical than most people suspected? She's still here, Kit. Older, maybe wiser in some ways, definitely more careful than she used to be—but still ready to believe in the impossible.

I broke my promise to you. The one about never forgetting how to dream big. I let fear make me small, let disappointment teach me to expect less, let the practical voice in my head edit out all the adventures until my life looked nothing like the stories we used to plan together. I'm sorry for that. Not just sorry I disappointed you, but sorry I disappointed the version of myself who believed we really would explore every single everywhere there was.

But here's what I've learned: promises can be repaired. Dreams can be revived. It's never too late to become the person you were meant to be, even if the path to get there looks different than you originally imagined.

At least, I hope that's true. I hope it's not too late to salvage something from the wreckage of my careful life.

I don't know where you are now, or what your life looks like, or whether you remember a lonely library girl who used to plan impossible expeditions with you. But I know this: if you're reading this letter, then the magic is working. Real explorers do always find each other, just like you said they would.

I have so much to tell you about this journey, about the places I've been and the parts of myself I've found and the tools I've learned to use. But mostly I want to hear about your adventures. I want to know what wonders you've discovered, what maps you've drawn, what stories you've collected in all the years since we said goodbye.

I work at the Millbrook Public Library now. The same one where we used to plan our adventures all those years ago. It seems fitting, doesn't it? That I ended up as a keeper of stories, even if I forgot for a while that I was supposed to be living them too. If you want to find me, I'll be there, surrounded by books and possibilities, finally ready for that big adventure we always talked about.

Whether you write back or not, I want you to know: you changed my life twice. Once when we were children and you taught me to believe in magic, and once when I was forty-five and tasting memory fruit helped me remember that the magic was real.

Thank you for being the kind of friend who believed in the impossible. Thank you for making me promise to dream big. And thank you for waiting, all these years, in the spaces between possibility and memory, until I was ready to remember who we used to be.

Your fellow explorer of elsewhere, Elsie

P.S. - I still have the notebook you gave me. The leather-bound one with the compass rose on the cover. It's been waiting patiently all these years for someone brave enough to fill it with adventures. I think it's finally time.

CHAPTER 6

THE ROOM WITH THE DOOR THAT ISN'T

The doorway from the Archive led not to another fantastic realm, but to something far more unsettling: a room that looked exactly like her apartment.

Not similar to her apartment, not reminiscent of it, but precisely identical down to the worn spot on the Persian rug where she always set down her tea cup, the stack of unread novels on the side table, the way afternoon light slanted through the window and painted everything in shades of comfortable resignation. Even the air smelled right—lavender sachets and old books and the faint trace of Earl Grey that seemed to live permanently in her kitchen.

This has to be a trap. Her pulse quickened as she recognized the careful perfection of the replication. *Not malicious, but still a trap. The kind that catches you by offering exactly what you think you want.*

"This is impossible," Elsie said, though by now she should have learned to expect impossibility. She walked to the window and looked out, expecting impossible vistas. Instead, she saw Maple Street exactly as it should be: Mrs. Henderson's garden with its predictable marigolds, the oak tree she'd watched grow for twenty years, the mailman making his reliable Tuesday rounds.

"Possibility and impossibility," Minimus observed from her shoulder, voice carrying what might have been amusement, "appear to be more flexible concepts than your species typically assumes."

The room felt like a question posed in familiar furniture and comforting routine. Everything that had made her feel safe for so many years was here, arranged exactly as she'd left it, waiting for her to slip back into patterns that had shaped her careful life. The temptation was immediate and powerful—she could almost feel her reading chair's familiar embrace, could almost taste the comfort of a life where the most difficult decision was which book to read next.

She could do it, she realized. She could sit down in her reading chair, make tea, and pretend none of the realms had happened. The Atlas—she reached for her bag and found it wasn't there. Of course not. The magic had served its purpose, shown her what she needed to see, and now offered her the choice to return to safety with lessons learned but adventure concluded.

Just sit down, part of her whispered—not the harsh voice of her shadow self, but something softer and more seductive. *Just rest. You've learned enough, grown enough. Why risk more when you could have this perfect safety?*

For a moment, Elsie found herself actually moving toward the chair, drawn by its promise of familiar comfort. The cushions would curve around her just so, the side table would hold her tea at exactly the right height, the window would frame the same view she'd contemplated for twenty years. It would be easy. It would be safe.

But as her hand touched the chair's worn fabric, she realized something was wrong. The texture was perfect, the temperature exactly right, but it felt hollow somehow—like a photograph of comfort rather than comfort itself. Beautiful, precise, but somehow empty of the weight of actual living.

"Where's the door?" she asked, stepping back from the chair and looking around the room that was perfectly, exactly her apartment except for the absence of any way out.

"What door?" Minimus asked.

"The door I came through. The door back to the Archive, or forward to whatever comes next." She turned in a slow circle, examining every wall, but found only familiar geography: the bookshelf with her favorite novels, the small dining table where she ate solitary meals, the bedroom door that led to her single bed and sensible nightstand.

"Perhaps," Minimus suggested delicately, "the door you're looking for isn't the one you came through."

Before Elsie could ask what he meant, she heard something that made her heart skip: the sound of someone making tea in her kitchen. Not just anyone—she knew the rhythm of those movements, the particular way the kettle was handled, the soft clink of china that spoke of someone who treated tea-making as meditation rather than chore.

It can't be. It's impossible. They're in Portland, they probably don't even remember me, they certainly wouldn't be here, in this place that isn't even really here.

"Kit?" she called, voice catching on the name.

"In here," came the reply, and it was Kit's voice, warm and familiar and impossible. "Though I should warn you, I'm not entirely sure I exist."

The words hung in the air between them, and Elsie understood with sudden clarity that this wasn't the Kit who had moved to Portland at sixteen, but the Kit who lived in her heart and memory—every conversation they'd never had, every possibility they'd represented, given form in this magical space between worlds.

Elsie found herself frozen between the living room and kitchen, caught in the space between hope and wonder. She had been writing to Kit, dreaming of Kit, slowly accepting that Kit had been real—but she wasn't prepared for the essence of Kit to actually be here, in her apartment, making tea as if twenty-nine years and the boundary between memory and reality meant nothing at all.

The sound of water being poured over tea bags reached her ears, followed by the gentle scrape of a spoon against ceramic. Such ordinary sounds, but they carried the weight of a miracle she wasn't sure she was ready to receive.

"Are you going to come in, or are we going to have this conversation through the doorway?" Kit's voice carried the same amused warmth she remembered, the same gentle teasing that had always made her feel like she was part of an inside joke with the universe.

Elsie stepped into the kitchen and there Kit was, exactly as they should be and nothing like she'd expected. Older, obviously—forty-five looked good on them, with silver threading through hair that still refused to stay properly neat and laugh lines that spoke of a life spent finding joy in unexpected places. They wore clothes that somehow managed to look both practical and adventurous: well-worn jeans, a soft sweater the color of forest shadows, and boots that had clearly walked many interesting miles.

But the most remarkable thing about Kit was how solid they seemed. Not dream-like or ghostly, but completely present and real, standing at her stove and brewing tea with the unconscious competence of someone who belonged in the space.

When Kit turned to smile at her, Elsie felt something flutter and settle in her chest—not the desperate hope she'd carried for so long, but something quieter and more substantial. Recognition. Not just of Kit's face, though that was wonderfully familiar, but of the way they moved through space, the way they held their shoulders, the particular quality of attention they brought to simple tasks.

"You look good, Elsie," Kit said, creek-water eyes taking her in with the same careful observation she remembered. "Different. Like you've been on a journey."

"You're here," Elsie said stupidly, accepting the mug Kit offered her with hands that shook just slightly. The ceramic was warm against her palms, real and solid in a way that made the rest of the room seem more authentic by association. "You're actually here, in my kitchen, making tea."

My good mugs. They're using my good mugs, the ones I save for special occasions. As if this is—as if I'm—

Her brain refused to complete the thought.

"I'm somewhere," Kit agreed, settling into the chair across from her small kitchen table as if they'd been having tea together every Tuesday for the past three decades. The gesture was so natural, so right, that Elsie felt tears prick her eyes. "Though I'm not entirely convinced that 'here' means what we think it means. Are you familiar with the concept of liminal space?"

"Thresholds," Elsie said, taking a sip of perfectly brewed tea and trying not to think about how Kit remembered exactly how she liked it prepared. "Spaces between other spaces. Places where the normal rules don't quite apply."

"Exactly. I think that's where we are—in the space between your journey and your return, between the person you were and the person you're becoming. A room that looks like your apartment but exists somewhere between possibility and reality."

The explanation should have been unsettling, but instead Elsie found it oddly comforting. It gave her permission to stop questioning the metaphysics of the moment and simply be present in it. Kit was here, in whatever sense mattered, and they were having tea and conversation as if time hadn't passed, as if the distance between sixteen and forty-five was just another threshold to cross.

"I got your letters," Kit said gently, as if sensing her need for reassurance. "All of them, though perhaps not in the way you'd expect. Letters written to someone who might not be real have a way of finding their intended recipient, especially when they're written with as much honesty as yours were."

Heat rose in Elsie's cheeks, but it was the warmth of recognition rather than shame. "You read them?"

"Every word. The uncertainty in the first one, the emotional awakening in the second, the tender recognition in the third, the complete honesty in the fourth." Kit's smile was warm with approval, and Elsie felt something in her chest expand like a flower opening to sunlight. "You've been doing the work, Elsie. The hard, necessary work of becoming who you actually are instead of who you thought you should be."

They understand. They read my letters and they understand what I was trying to say, what I was trying to become.

Elsie sipped her tea—perfectly brewed, exactly as she liked it—and tried to process the impossibility of the moment. The kitchen around them seemed to pulse gently with warmth and possibility, as if responding to the connection being rebuilt between them.

"Are you real? Are you really Kit, or are you something this place created to help me work through my feelings about losing you?"

"Does it matter?" Kit asked, voice carrying the same philosophical curiosity she remembered from their childhood debates. They leaned forward slightly, elbows on the table in a gesture so familiar it made her breath catch. "If I help you understand something true about yourself, if this conversation changes how you see your life and your choices, does the metaphysical status of my existence affect the value of what we discover together?"

"I suppose not," Elsie said slowly, though part of her still craved certainty. "But I need to know—for my own sanity, if nothing else. Are you the Kit who moved to Portland when we were sixteen? Are you the person I've been writing to?"

Kit considered this, hands wrapped around their mug in a gesture so familiar it made Elsie's chest ache with recognition. Steam rose from their tea, creating brief, shifting patterns in the air between them—ephemeral and beautiful and impossible to hold.

"I'm the Kit who lives in your heart," they said finally, voice gentle with understanding. "I'm the Kit who represents everything you've ever known about courage and possibility and the willingness to believe in magic. Whether that Kit corresponds to a flesh-and-blood person living in Portland is a different question entirely."

"That's not an answer."

"It's the only answer I can give you from inside this liminal space," Kit said, their smile carrying both apology and invitation. "But I can tell you this: the lessons you learned in the realms were real. The tools you gathered, the parts of yourself you reclaimed, the integration you achieved with your shadow—all of that actually happened, regardless of whether I'm sitting in a kitchen in Portland right now wondering why I keep thinking about a childhood friend named Elsie."

The kitchen around them seemed to shimmer slightly, as if it couldn't decide whether it was more real or more metaphor. Through the window, Maple Street wavered between the familiar neighborhood she knew and something that looked like the view from a ship sailing on seas of possibility.

But what if I'm not ready? The thought arose with sudden intensity, and Elsie found herself looking longingly toward the living room where her reading chair waited with its promise of familiar safety. *What if I choose the adventure and I can't handle it? What if I reach out to the real you and you don't want me to find you?*

For a moment, the temptation to retreat was overwhelming. She could finish this cup of tea, say goodbye to this version of Kit, and settle into her chair with a book and the comfortable certainty of an unchanged life. The adventure could end here, with lessons learned but risks still safely avoided.

The chair seemed to call to her from the next room, offering the embrace of the known, the comfort of limitations freely chosen rather than imposed. She could almost feel the familiar weight of a book in her lap, the satisfaction of problems that existed only on pages and could be solved by turning to the back.

"What happens now?" Elsie asked, voice smaller than she'd intended. "Do I wake up in my bed and discover this was all an elaborate dream? Do I go back to my library job and pretend none of this happened?"

Kit must have seen something in her expression—the pull toward safety, the old familiar fear—because they set down their mug and reached across the table to cover her hand with theirs. Their touch was warm, solid, entirely present.

"That's up to you," they said, leaning forward with the intensity she remembered from their childhood planning sessions. "That's what this room is really about—it's not the absence of a door, it's the presence of choice. You can stay here, in this safe replica of your comfortable life, or you can create the door that leads to whatever comes next."

The weight of Kit's hand on hers anchored her to the moment, to the choice being offered. Real or not, Kit was here, believing in her capacity to choose growth over safety, adventure over comfort. The same Kit who had always seen possibilities where she saw only obstacles.

"Create a door? How?"

Kit's smile was radiant with the same confidence that had always made impossible things seem achievable. "The same way you've been creating everything else on this journey—by choosing who you want to be and then becoming that person. By deciding what story you want to live and then having the courage to write it."

As if in response to Kit's words, the room around them began to shift. Not dramatically—the furniture remained the same, the layout unchanged—but somehow everything felt more possible, more alive with potential. The books on her shelves seemed to glow with stories waiting to be read, the window showed vistas that extended beyond any single neighborhood, and the air itself hummed with the energy of decisions waiting to be made.

But still, the reading chair called to her. Still, the safe path beckoned with its promise of a life without risk, without the possibility of devastating failure or rejection.

"I'm scared," Elsie admitted, fingers tightening around her mug. "What if I choose wrong? What if I try to live this bigger life and I fail? What if I reach out to the real you and you don't remember me, or don't care?"

"Then you'll have tried," Kit said simply, their thumb tracing gentle circles on the back of her hand. "Then you'll have stories to tell, even if they're stories about failure. Then you'll have lived fully enough to have something worth remembering."

The echo of her own words from the Archive made Elsie smile despite her fear. Even if Kit was a projection of her own psyche, they were a projection that knew her well enough to reflect her own hard-won wisdom back to her.

"Besides," Kit continued, voice taking on the teasing tone she remembered from childhood, "what makes you think failing at something you care about is worse than succeeding at something you don't? What makes you think a messy, uncertain life full of attempts and adventures is less valuable than a tidy, predictable life full of safety and sameness?"

The safety is an illusion anyway. I've been trying to control outcomes by avoiding choices, but that's not actually safety—it's just a different kind of risk. The risk of reaching the end of my life and realizing I never really lived it.

She looked around the kitchen that was both hers and not hers, at the person who was both Kit and the idea of Kit, at the choice that was both simple and impossibly complex. She thought about the realms she'd traveled, the tools she'd gathered, the parts of herself she'd reclaimed. She thought about the memory seed in her pocket and the emotional mirror that showed her the weather of her own heart.

The reading chair still beckoned from the next room, but its call was fainter now, competing with a different kind of invitation—the invitation to discover what lay beyond the safety of the familiar.

"I want to try," she said, and the words carried more weight than she'd expected. They seemed to resonate in the air around them, creating ripples of possibility that she could almost see. "I want to write the stories I've been afraid to write. I want to take the risks I've been avoiding. I want to plant the seed Mira gave me and see what grows from intentions backed by action."

"And?" Kit prompted gently, eyes bright with encouragement.

"And I want to find you. The real you, if you exist. I want to send a letter to Portland and see what happens. I want to fill that notebook you gave me with adventures and discoveries and moments that make Tuesday afternoons feel like chapters in an epic story."

As she spoke, something remarkable happened. A door began to appear on the blank wall behind Kit—not materializing all at once, but sketching itself into existence line by line, as if drawn by an invisible hand responding to her growing certainty. The process was beautiful to watch, like watching an artist work, each stroke adding definition and possibility to what had been empty space.

"There's your door," Kit said, turning to look at it with satisfaction. "Made from intention and courage and the willingness to author your own story instead of letting fear do the writing."

The door was beautiful—not ornate, but somehow perfect. Warm wood with brass hinges that seemed to glow with their own inner light, a handle that invited touch, proportions that suggested it might lead anywhere and everywhere. Above it, words were writing themselves in familiar script: *The Return to Authoring*.

Through the emerging threshold, Elsie could see not another impossible realm, but something even more magical: the ordinary world transformed by the possibility of being lived fully. Her library, but somehow brighter, alive with the rustle of pages that wanted to be turned and the whisper of stories that needed to be told. Patrons moved between the stacks not just seeking information, but hunting for the kind of books that changed lives.

Her apartment was visible too, but expanded by the knowledge that home could be a launching point for adventures rather than a hiding place from them. The familiar rooms glowed with new possibility—the kitchen where she might cook meals for friends, the living room where she might write late into the night, the bedroom where she might dream of tomorrow's adventures rather than yesterday's regrets.

"Will you come with me?" Elsie asked, though she already knew the answer.

"I'll always be with you," Kit said, standing and moving toward the door. "In every choice you make to be brave instead of safe, in every moment you choose growth over comfort, in every story you decide to live instead of just imagine. But the walking has to be yours, Elsie. That's how authorship works—you have to be the one who turns the pages."

Kit reached the door first and turned back to her with a smile that contained all the warmth and encouragement she'd ever needed. The light from the threshold caught the silver in their hair, made their eyes seem to hold depths of understanding that hadn't been there when they were sixteen.

"Are you ready?"

Elsie stood, leaving her empty teacup on the table beside Kit's, and realized that she was. Not ready in the sense of having everything figured out, not ready in the sense of feeling certain about what would happen next, but ready in the sense of being willing to find out. Ready to exchange the safety of the known for the adventure of the possible.

Behind her, the reading chair made one final, gentle appeal—not demanding, but offering. The life of comfortable routine, of questions that stayed safely theoretical, of dreams that remained pristine because they were never tested against reality.

I'm sorry, she thought toward it, feeling genuine gratitude for all the comfort it had provided over the years. *But I'm ready for a different kind of comfort now. The comfort of knowing I'm living my own life instead of hiding from it.*

"Yes," she said, voice clear with decision. "I'm ready to start writing my own story."

Kit opened the door, and the light that spilled through was warm and golden, carrying the scent of fresh possibilities and new adventures. It smelled like library books and ink and tea, but also like rain on unfamiliar streets and the salt air of coastlines she'd never seen.

"After you," Kit said, gesturing toward the doorway with a grace that made the simple act seem ceremonial. "Real explorers always know how to find each other, remember? I'll be waiting for you to catch up."

Elsie stepped toward the door, carrying with her the taste of perfectly brewed tea and the knowledge that some conversations change everything, even when you're not entirely sure who you're talking to. Behind her, the safe replica of her apartment began to fade, its job complete. The reading chair dissolved with the rest of it, but she felt no loss—only anticipation for the stories she would write in the real world, stories that would require no chair at all but only the courage to live them.

The threshold felt warm under her feet as she crossed it, and somewhere in the distance—or perhaps very close—she could hear the sound of pages turning, as if the room held the hush of a page about to turn.

Minimus, still perched on her shoulder, adjusted his tiny grip and cleared his throat. "Well," he said with satisfaction, "that was considerably more philosophically complex than I expected. Shall we see what story you write next?"

"Yes," Elsie said, stepping through the door into the light beyond, carrying with her the memory of Kit's smile and the promise of a life authored by courage instead of fear. "Let's see what happens when someone finally decides to become the hero of their own adventure."

The door closed gently behind them, not with finality but with the soft sound of a book closing on one chapter so that another might begin.

CHAPTER 7

THE HOUSE OF UNFINISHED STORIES

The door that Elsie had authored with intention and courage led not back to her familiar library, but to the most extraordinary building she had ever seen. It was a house, but one that seemed to have been designed by someone who understood that stories, like living things, require room to grow and change and surprise their creators.

The structure sprawled in all directions without any apparent plan, as if rooms had been added whenever someone needed space for a particular kind of narrative. Gothic towers twisted skyward next to cozy cottage chambers, Victorian bay windows jutted out from walls that also featured sleek modernist glass panels, and staircases led in directions that should have been geometrically impossible but somehow felt perfectly logical.

It's like looking at the outside of someone's mind. Her chest tightened with recognition. *All the different ways we try to contain our stories, all the different architectures we build around our dreams.*

"The House of Unfinished Stories," Minimus said from her shoulder, voice carrying professional interest. "I've heard of this place but never seen it. Supposedly, every room contains a narrative that someone started but never completed."

As they approached the front door—a massive oak portal that looked borrowed from a medieval castle—Elsie could hear something that made her heart race: the sound of stories being told. Not out loud, but in the way that stories speak when they're actively being lived rather than passively consumed. The rustle of pages that turned themselves, the whisper of words writing themselves across empty space, the soft sigh of characters discovering what they were capable of.

The door opened before she could knock, revealing a figure that seemed composed entirely of ink and possibility. It wore the shape of an elderly woman, but its edges shifted and flowed like manuscript text that hadn't quite settled into final form.

"Welcome, author," it said, and its voice carried the rhythm of stories that knew their own worth. "I am the Keeper of Unfinished Things. You arrive at a most fortuitous moment—we have a story that has been waiting decades for someone brave enough to complete it."

"I'm not sure I understand," Elsie said, though part of her was beginning to suspect she understood perfectly, and the understanding was more overwhelming than she was ready to admit. The word 'author' sat strangely in her chest—not uncomfortable, exactly, but unfamiliar, like trying on clothes in a style she'd never worn before.

The Keeper smiled, and when it did, words appeared briefly in the air around its face before dissolving back into possibility. "Every story that someone begins but leaves incomplete finds its way here eventually. They wait patiently, these narrative orphans, hoping that someday their creator—or someone with courage to adopt them— will give them the ending they deserve."

It gestured for them to follow, leading them through corridors lined with doors of every description. Some were firmly closed, sealed with what looked like wax or regret. Others stood slightly ajar, leaking fragments of conversation and description into the hallway. A few were wide open, inviting completion, their stories so eager to be finished that they practically pulled at Elsie as she passed.

"How many stories are here?" she asked, overwhelmed by the sheer number of doors stretching in every direction.

"All of them," the Keeper replied simply. "Every novel someone started during November but abandoned by December. Every poem that stalled at the second verse. Every love letter that was written but never sent. Every dream that someone began to pursue but set aside when life became complicated."

They passed a room where she could see a ghostly figure sitting at a typewriter, pecking away at keys that made no sound and produced no words on paper. The sight hit Elsie like a physical blow to the chest.

That could be me. That's exactly what I've been doing—going through the motions of writing, of living, but never actually creating anything real. Never finishing anything that mattered.

Through another doorway, she glimpsed someone pacing endlessly, clearly stuck on a plot point they couldn't resolve. The figure's face was a mask of frustration and self-doubt, and Elsie recognized the expression from her own mirror on too many mornings when she'd woken with the weight of unfinished projects pressing down on her chest.

In a third room, a writer sat surrounded by crumpled papers, each one containing the first paragraph of what might have been a masterpiece.

How many first pages have I written? How many beginnings have I abandoned the moment they started to require real commitment, real risk?

"It's heartbreaking," Elsie murmured, voice thick with recognition and regret.

"It's hopeful," the Keeper corrected gently. "Every unfinished story is an act of faith—faith that someday, somehow, it will find its proper conclusion. They don't consider themselves failures. They consider themselves works in progress."

Works in progress. The phrase settled in Elsie's chest with the weight of possibility. Not failures, not mistakes, not evidence of inadequacy—just stories that hadn't found their endings yet.

The Keeper stopped before a door that was neither closed nor fully open, but seemed to hover in a state of potential. Above it, words appeared and disappeared like thoughts on the edge of consciousness: *The Adventures of Two Young Explorers* and *Letters Never Sent* and *The Promise Keepers* and finally, settling into clarity: *The Story of Kit and Elsie.*

"Ah," Elsie breathed, her heart stuttering with recognition that felt both inevitable and impossible.

"This story began when you were children," the Keeper explained, "but it stalled when you were sixteen and fear convinced you that some stories were too risky to continue. It's been waiting here ever since, hoping that someday its co-author would find the courage to write the next chapter."

The door opened at Elsie's approach, revealing a room that contained every conversation she and Kit had ever had, every plan they'd made, every promise they'd sworn to keep. She could see their twelve-year-old selves bent over fairy tale books, mapping expeditions to impossible places. Their fourteen-year-old selves reading poetry by the creek, making vows about never forgetting how to dream big. Their sixteen-year-old selves saying goodbye, with Kit pressing that leather-bound notebook into her hands and making her promise to keep exploring.

But the room also contained something else: all the years of silence that had followed. All the letters she hadn't written, all the adventures she hadn't taken, all the ways she had let fear edit their story into incompleteness. The weight of all that absence pressed against her ribs like held breath.

I did this. I'm the one who decided our story was too risky to continue.

I'm the one who chose safety over connection, certainty over possibility. But that means I'm also the one who can choose differently.

"It's not just my story to finish," Elsie said, voice small but growing stronger with each word. "Kit would have to participate. Kit would have to want to continue the story."

"Would they?" the Keeper asked, and there was something almost playful in the question, as if the answer was more obvious than Elsie was allowing herself to believe. "If Kit existed, if Kit remembered the promises you made, if Kit had spent these years wondering what became of the girl who was going to explore impossible places—would they want to write the next chapter with you?"

Elsie thought about the Kit she had just been talking with in her kitchen, whether that Kit was metaphor or memory or somehow the real person reaching across impossible distances. She thought about the confidence in Kit's voice when they said *Real explorers always know how to find each other*, the way their presence had felt both strange and completely natural.

The memory of Kit's hand covering hers came back with startling clarity—the warmth of that touch, the way it had anchored her to the moment and to the choice she needed to make.

"I think..." she began, then paused, feeling the weight of what she was about to commit to. The words seemed to hover on the edge of speech, requiring a kind of courage she wasn't sure she possessed. "I think they might. But I don't know how to reach them. I don't know if they're real, or where they are, or if they even remember me the way I remember them."

The Keeper smiled, and this time the words that appeared around its face stayed visible long enough to read: *Stories have their own gravity. They pull their characters toward completion.*

"Enter the room," the Keeper suggested. "Become part of the story you abandoned. See what happens when you're willing to participate in your own narrative instead of just observing it from a safe distance."

Elsie hesitated on the threshold, hand gripping the doorframe.

This is the moment. This is where I either step into my own story or stay safely outside it, watching other people live their lives while I catalog and organize and maintain everyone else's adventures.

She took a breath that seemed to come from somewhere deeper than her lungs, and stepped across the threshold.

Immediately, she felt the difference. This wasn't like entering the other realms, where she had been a visitor experiencing someone else's magical territory. This was like stepping into her own life, but a version of her life where possibility had never been edited out by fear.

The room expanded around her, showing not just the past they had shared, but the futures they might create. She saw herself writing in the notebook Kit had given her, filling it with descriptions of the realms she had visited and the tools she had learned to use. The image was so vivid she could almost feel the pen in her hand, the satisfying weight of words accumulating on the page.

She saw Kit opening a letter with her return address, their face lighting up with the same joy she remembered from childhood. The vision was so clear she could see the expression of delighted surprise, the way Kit's eyes would widen before crinkling into that familiar smile.

She saw conversations over tea, shared adventures through both impossible realms and ordinary Tuesday afternoons that felt magical because they were lived with attention and intention. She could almost hear their voices, older now but carrying the same rhythms of connection and understanding she remembered.

But she also saw the risks. The possibility that Kit might not remember her fondly, or might have grown into someone too different from the child she had known. The chance that their rekindled friendship might disappoint them both, failing to live up to the mythic proportions it had assumed in memory. The reality that some stories, no matter how beautiful their beginning, weren't meant to have the endings their characters originally envisioned.

Even disappointment is a story. Even failure teaches you something about the shape of your hopes. The only real failure would be never finding out.

"I see the possibilities," she said to the room, addressing both the Keeper and the story itself. Her voice was steadier now, carrying the authority of someone who had learned to read the weather of her own heart. "Both the beautiful ones and the painful ones. I see that finishing this story means risking disappointment, rejection, the discovery that some promises can't be kept even when you find the courage to try."

The room pulsed around her, waiting for her decision. She could feel the story itself holding its breath, poised between completion and eternal suspension.

"But I also see that not finishing the story means living with the certainty of incompletion," she continued, voice growing stronger with conviction. "It means accepting that fear gets to write the ending instead of courage. It means letting the best parts of who I was—who we were—remain forever frozen in childhood instead of growing into what they might become."

She reached into her pocket and withdrew the memory seed Mira had given her, the one that contained potential for experiences yet to be lived. As she held it, the room around her shifted again, showing her something new: Kit in Portland, sitting at a desk in what looked like an independent bookstore, surrounded by maps and travel guides and journals filled with observations about the places where magic still lived in the ordinary world.

But this Kit looked up suddenly, as if hearing their name called from a great distance, and smiled with recognition that crossed whatever boundaries existed between memory and reality, between story and life.

"That's not just possibility," Elsie realized, heart racing with the certainty of connection. "That's happening right now. Somewhere, somehow, Kit is thinking about me at exactly the moment I'm thinking about them."

The Keeper appeared beside her, its form more solid now, more invested in the outcome of this particular story. "Some narratives," it said, "have their own momentum. Some connections transcend the ordinary limitations of time and space and the question of who is real versus who is metaphor. The question isn't whether Kit exists—it's whether you're brave enough to act as if they do."

Act as if they do. The phrase settled in her chest like a key finding its lock. She didn't need certainty about Kit's existence—she just needed the courage to behave as if connection were possible, as if stories could bridge decades and distance and the accumulated caution of middle age.

Elsie looked around the room one more time, seeing all the versions of their story that were possible: the one where she remained safe and forever wondering, the one where she reached out and discovered beautiful connection, the one where she tried and faced disappointment but learned something valuable about courage in the process.

All of them were better than the version where she never tried at all.

"I want to finish the story," she said, and her voice carried the authority of someone who had finally decided to become the author of her own life. "Not just this story, but all the stories I've left incomplete. I want to write in the notebook Kit gave me. I want to send a letter to Portland. I want to plant this seed and see what grows from intentions backed by action."

As she spoke, something extraordinary happened. The room began to write itself around her words, filling in details and possibilities as if her commitment to completion was giving the story permission to unfold. She could see the letter she would write, honest and vulnerable and hopeful. She could see herself addressing it to bookstores in Portland, trusting that if Kit was meant to receive it, the universe would find a way to deliver it.

She could see the notebook filling with observations and adventures, becoming not just a record of journeys taken but an invitation for journeys yet to come. She could see the seed planted in soil enriched by intention, growing into experiences that would surprise and delight the person who chose to live them fully.

But most remarkably, she could see Kit—not as a memory or a metaphor, but as a living person opening a letter with growing excitement, recognizing the handwriting before they even saw the signature, smiling with the same joy that had lit up their face when they discovered a particularly promising doorway to adventure.

"Stories," the Keeper said with satisfaction as the room settled into its new configuration of completion, "have their own ways of making themselves true."

The room had transformed around them. No longer a repository of abandoned narrative, it had become a launching point for stories that were ready to be lived. The walls showed not just possibilities but probabilities, not just dreams but plans backed by courage and sweetened by the willingness to risk disappointment in service of growth.

"What happens now?" Elsie asked, though she thought she already knew the answer.

"Now you write," the Keeper said simply. "You go back to your library, but you go as an author instead of just a curator. You tend to other people's stories while actively living your own. You learn that the most important books are sometimes the ones you write with your choices rather than your pen."

A new door had appeared in the room, leading not to another impossible realm but to something even more magical: her ordinary life transformed by the knowledge that adventure was always available to those who were willing to see it, seek it, and sometimes create it from nothing more than intention and hope.

"Will I see you again?" she asked the Keeper as they prepared to part.

"Every time you finish something you started," the Keeper replied. "Every time you choose completion over abandonment, growth over safety, the uncertain beauty of attempting over the certain emptiness of not trying. Every time you remember that you are the author of your own story, I am there in the margins, cheering you on."

Elsie moved toward the door that would take her home, but home to a life she was finally ready to live fully. Behind her, the House of Unfinished Stories settled into quiet contentment, its halls a little brighter now that another narrative had found its way toward completion.

In her pocket, the memory seed pulsed with warm potential, and in her heart, she carried the knowledge that some promises could be kept even decades after they were made, some friendships could survive the geography of time and fear and the accumulated caution that came with learning how much it was possible to lose.

"Thank you," she said to the house itself, to the stories that had waited patiently for their endings, to the parts of herself that had never stopped believing in the possibility of happy conclusions earned through courage rather than granted through luck.

The door opened onto familiar territory made new by the willingness to see it with fresh eyes. Her journey through impossible realms was complete, but her journey as the conscious author of her own adventure was just beginning.

And somewhere in Portland, a person who might be Kit looked up from their work with sudden, inexplicable hope, as if they had just heard their name called by a voice they had been waiting thirty years to hear again.

The story was no longer unfinished. It was simply ready for its next chapter.

INTERLUDE #5: LETTER TO KIT

Written on the first page of a transformed atlas, the handwriting confident and flowing, as if the act of writing itself has become a form of magic.

My Dear Kit,

I'm writing this on the first page of what used to be an impossible book and has now become something even more extraordinary: a space for me to document the adventures I choose to live rather than the ones that happen to me.

I don't know who you are yet—not in the practical sense of where you live or what your life looks like or whether the Kit I've been writing to corresponds to a flesh-and-blood person walking around in Portland. But I know what you mean to me, and that feels like the most important truth I've discovered in forty-five years of careful living.

Which might be the most important truth, or might be elaborate self-deception. But I'm choosing to believe it's the former.

You mean courage that doesn't require fearlessness. You mean the part of me that never learned to apologize for wanting impossible things. You mean the voice that says "the best adventures begin when you stop worrying about being ready" and actually believes it enough to act on it.

Whether you exist as a person I can write actual letters to or as the embodiment of everything I've ever known about wonder and possibility, you've been my compass through territories I never imagined I was brave enough to explore. You've been the voice reminding me that small thoughts can grow large enough to live in, that emotions are tools rather than weather, that courage is always available as a choice rather than a feeling.

I've just done something that would have been impossible when I started writing these letters: I gave away magic in order to trust the magic I've become. I had the chance to keep a book that could transport me to impossible realms whenever ordinary life became too difficult to navigate, and I chose instead to believe that the real magic was never in the book—it was in what the book helped me remember about my own capacity for transformation.

I'm not telling you this to prove how brave I've become. I'm telling you because I understand now that courage isn't a destination you reach—it's a muscle you strengthen through use. And I want to keep strengthening it, want to keep choosing growth over safety, possibility over predictability, the uncertain beauty of attempting over the certain emptiness of not trying.

I'm going to mail this letter, Kit. Not to the uncertain space between memory and metaphor where I've been sending these other letters, but to actual bookstores in Portland, with your actual name on the envelope. Because even if you don't exist, even if you don't remember me, even if this letter never finds its way to the person it's meant for, the act of sending it is itself an adventure worth taking.

And because I can't keep writing letters to my own imagina-

tion forever. At some point, you have to risk actual contact with actual reality.

I'm going to fill the notebook you gave me all those years ago. Not with apologies for the time I wasted or explanations for why I chose safety over our shared dreams, but with descriptions of the magic I'm learning to create through my choices. The way Tuesday afternoons become adventures when lived with attention. The way helping library patrons find exactly the book they didn't know they needed becomes a form of cartography, mapping the territories of the human heart.

I'm going to plant the memory seed I was given in a realm where memories grow like fruit on impossible trees. I'm going to water it with intention and tend it with the kind of attention I used to reserve for other people's stories, and see what grows from the soil of a life consciously chosen.

Most importantly, I'm going to stop editing myself out of my own story. I'm going to stop letting the voice that says "be practical, be safe, don't risk disappointment" make all the important decisions. I'm going to write myself back into the narrative of my own life, not as a supporting character in other people's adventures, but as the author of experiences worth remembering.

If you're real—if you're sitting in a bookstore in Portland, surrounded by maps and travel guides and journals filled with observations about where magic still lives in the ordinary world—I hope this letter finds you. I hope it arrives at exactly the moment when you most need to remember that some promises can be kept even decades after they're made, that some friendships transcend the ordinary limitations of time and space and the question of who exists where.

If you're not real in the way that requires a physical address and a postal system—if you're something my heart created to represent everything I've ever known about wonder and possibility—then this letter is still for you. It's proof that the lessons you taught me about dreaming big and staying curious and never apologizing for wanting impossible things have taken root in soil that's finally ready to support them.

Either way, I want you to know: you changed my life. Not once, but twice. First when we were children and you showed me that the world was far more magical than most people suspected, and again now, when writing to you helped me remember that the magic was always mine to claim.

I'm ready now, Kit. Ready for the adventure we always talked about, whether it's exploring impossible realms or discovering that Tuesday afternoons can be magical when approached with the right mixture of attention and intention. Ready to be someone who authors her own story rather than just curating other people's narratives.

Ready to be the kind of person who writes letters to old friends without knowing for certain they'll be received, who plants seeds without guaranteeing they'll grow, who chooses possibility over safety even when safety feels so much more predictable and comfortable.

I don't know what comes next, but for the first time in decades, that uncertainty feels like a gift rather than a threat. Because I understand now that the best adventures begin not with detailed maps and careful plans, but with the simple, radical decision to trust that you're capable of navigating whatever territory you discover.

Real explorers always know how to find each other, you told me once. I'm finally ready to find out if you were right.

With all my love and gratitude and newly-claimed courage,

Elsie

P.S. - I'm including my address at the library, because if you exist and this letter finds you, I want you to know exactly where I'll be: surrounded by stories and possibilities, finally ready to live an adventure worthy of documentation. The door is always open for fellow explorers, especially ones who remember that the most important maps are the ones that lead not to places, but to the unexplored territories of a life consciously chosen.

And below that, almost as an afterthought: "P.P.S. - I still have the compass rose notebook. It's time to fill it with adventures."

CHAPTER 8

THE RETURN SPIRAL

The door from the House of Unfinished Stories opened not onto her library as Elsie had expected, but onto a spiral staircase that seemed to wind both upward and downward simultaneously, defying geometry in favor of something that felt more like the logic of dreams.

Each step she took seemed to echo not just in the immediate space, but through all the realms she had visited. She could hear the Inch-High Philosophers debating the philosophical implications of her footsteps, could feel the emotional landscape of Sym's realm responding to her mixture of anticipation and uncertainty, could smell the memory fruit growing more fragrant as she approached what felt like both an ending and a beginning.

Where the hell am I now?

"This is a return spiral," Minimus observed from her shoulder, voice carrying scientific fascination mixed with what might have been affection. "A space designed to help travelers integrate their experiences before re-entering ordinary reality. Each step allows you to process what you've learned and choose what aspects of your journey you want to carry forward consciously."

The staircase was beautiful in a way that seemed specifically crafted for her aesthetic sensibilities—not grand or imposing, but thoughtfully designed, with banisters that felt perfect under her palm and steps that gave slightly under her feet as if they were made of compressed possibilities rather than ordinary stone. The walls were lined with niches, each one containing objects that seemed to represent different aspects of her journey: a tiny chair from the Cartographer's realm, a vial of shifting colors that captured the essence of Sym's emotional teachings, a pressed flower from the Memory Orchard, a page covered with writing that appeared and disappeared.

"Why a spiral?" she asked, though she suspected she already knew the answer.

"Because journeys of transformation aren't linear," came a familiar voice from above. "Because sometimes you have to circle back to where you started to understand how far you've traveled."

Elsie looked up to see the Cartographer of Comfort descending toward her, but this version seemed different—less angular, more integrated, as if it had absorbed something essential from witnessing her journey.

The Cartographer looks different too. More solid somehow, more present. Does everyone who serves as a guide get transformed by the process?

"You've returned to the beginning," the Cartographer said as they met on a landing that seemed to exist specifically for this conversation. "But not the same beginning you left. You understand now that The Chair Room wasn't about choosing between sitting and traveling—it was about learning that true comfort comes not from avoiding challenge, but from building the skills to navigate it wisely."

Around them, the spiral staircase opened into a circular space that Elsie recognized as a transformed version of the original Chair Room. The chairs were still there, but they no longer spoke of limitation or stagnation. Instead, they seemed to represent different kinds of rest, different ways of gathering strength for the next adventure. Reading chairs positioned to catch the best light for studying maps, meditation cushions arranged for the kind of quiet reflection that preceded wise action, writing desks equipped with everything needed to document discoveries and plan future explorations.

"It's beautiful," Elsie said, understanding flooding through her as she saw how the space had evolved in response to her own growth. "The chairs aren't prisons anymore. They're... tools. Places to prepare and reflect and gather energy."

"Exactly," the Cartographer said with approval. "You've learned that rest and adventure aren't opposites—they're partners. One makes the other possible."

But Elsie's attention was drawn to the center of the room, where something both familiar and heartbreaking waited for her: the Atlas itself, sitting open on a simple wooden table, its pages glowing with warm light she had come to associate with possibility and transformation.

Her chest tightened with sudden understanding, a flutter of panic rising beneath her ribs.

Oh no. Oh shit. I know what this is.

"The final test," she said, recognizing the moment even as she dreaded it.

"Not a test," the Cartographer corrected gently. "A gift. The Atlas has served its purpose for you—it has shown you the territories of your own heart, helped you reclaim the parts of yourself you had lost or buried, taught you that courage and wisdom and emotional honesty are tools you can learn to use consciously. Now it's time to decide what happens next."

A gift that requires giving something away. The kind of gift that asks you to prove you've learned what you think you've learned.

Elsie approached the table slowly, her heart heavy with understanding. She had known this moment would come—had known even as she first opened the impossible book that eventually she would have to choose between keeping the magic and trusting that she had internalized its lessons.

The Atlas lay open before her, its pages shimmering with invitations to realms she'd never seen, territories that promised new adventures and continued transformation. Part of her wanted to reach out and turn the page, to lose herself in another impossible journey rather than face the weight of returning to ordinary life.

"I have to give it up," she said, not quite making it a question. Her voice came out smaller than she'd intended, betraying the depth of her reluctance.

"You have to choose," the Cartographer replied, and Elsie caught something in its tone—not indifference, but a kind of gentle compassion that suggested it understood exactly what it was asking of her. "You can keep the Atlas, return to your library, and always know that magic is available to you when ordinary life becomes too difficult to navigate. You would be safe, always able to escape when reality becomes overwhelming."

The offer was tempting in ways that went deeper than simple desire for the fantastic. The Atlas represented certainty—certain magic, certain escape, certain proof that she was special enough to deserve extraordinary experiences. Keeping it would mean never having to fully trust her own growth, never having to believe completely in her ability to create magic through her choices rather than access it through supernatural means.

And I could keep having adventures. I could explore every realm that exists, become someone who lives permanently in the magical rather than just visiting it. No more ordinary Tuesday afternoons, no more small disappointments and everyday worries. Just constant wonder and transformation.

"But," the Cartographer continued, watching her face with careful attention, "there is another option. You can release the Atlas to find its next bearer—someone else who needs to learn what you have learned—and trust that the real magic was never in the book itself, but in what it helped you remember about your own capacity for transformation."

Trust. The word settled in her chest like a stone. After spending her entire adult life avoiding situations that required trust—in herself, in others, in the fundamental goodness of uncertainty—she was being asked to make the ultimate act of faith.

"And if I'm wrong?" Elsie asked, voice barely above a whisper. The question carried all her deepest fears, all the old certainties about her own limitations that she'd been working to overcome. "What if I give it away and discover that without it, I'm just... ordinary? What if the courage and wisdom I think I've gained were just temporary effects of being in magical realms, and without that external support, I revert to being the careful, small person I was before?"

The Cartographer's expression softened with understanding, and Elsie realized that this question—this exact fear—was probably voiced by every traveler who reached this point. The doubt wasn't a sign of failure; it was a natural part of the process.

"Then you would learn something valuable about the nature of true transformation," the Cartographer said, voice carrying both honesty and encouragement. "And you would discover whether the person you've become during this journey is strong enough to continue growing without magical assistance."

But what if the answer is no? The thought rose unbidden, carrying with it images of herself six months from now, back to hiding behind other people's stories, too afraid to write the letter to Kit, the memory seed forgotten in a drawer somewhere. *What if I'm not as changed as I think I am?*

Minimus shifted on her shoulder, his tiny weight somehow comforting in its steadiness. "If I may offer a beetle's perspective," he said thoughtfully, "the most significant changes you've undergone have been internal. The Atlas provided the context and catalyst for your growth, but the actual work—the choices, the integration, the courage to face your shadow self—that all came from you."

Elsie looked down at the open Atlas, its pages showing not the realms she had visited, but new territories she had never seen—vast landscapes of possibility that seemed to extend beyond the boundaries of any single person's journey. She realized that the book had changed as she had changed, that it was no longer specifically hers but had evolved into something ready to serve whatever traveler needed it next.

Her hand moved toward the pages almost without conscious direction, drawn by the promise of continued magic, continued certainty that she was someone special enough to deserve extraordinary experiences. But as her fingers approached the glowing paper, she hesitated, feeling the weight of everything she'd learned about the difference between true security and the illusion of safety.

"There's someone else, isn't there?" she said, understanding blooming in her chest. "Someone else who needs to learn that courage is a choice, that emotions are tools, that it's never too late to reclaim the parts of yourself you've lost."

"There is always someone else," the Cartographer confirmed. "The Atlas finds its way to people when they're ready for transformation, when the gap between who they are and who they're capable of becoming has grown large enough to create the gravitational pull necessary for real change."

Elsie thought about her journey, about the scared librarian who had first touched the Atlas's pages and been transported into the impossible. That person felt both intimately familiar and almost unrecognizably distant—still herself, but a version of herself that had been limited by fears she now understood were choices rather than immutable facts about her character.

She thought about the tools she had gathered: the understanding that scale was about what you measured against, the knowledge that emotions were information rather than weather, the courage to face and integrate her shadow self, the commitment to authoring her own story rather than letting fear do the writing. These weren't magical artifacts that could be taken away—they were skills, perspectives, ways of being in the world that belonged to her now regardless of whether she had access to impossible realms.

Her hand was still hovering over the Atlas, trembling slightly with the magnitude of the choice. She could feel the pull of the magical pages, the promise they offered of continued adventures and constant wonder. But she could also feel something else—the pull of the real world, not as a place of limitation but as a territory waiting to be explored with all the tools she'd gained.

What would it mean to approach my ordinary life with the same sense of adventure I brought to impossible realms? What would it mean to write that letter to Kit not as someone hoping for magical intervention, but as someone who understands that connection itself is the deepest magic?

"I think," she said slowly, hand still hovering over the Atlas's open pages, "I'm ready to trust that the magic was always mine. But I'm terrified that I'm wrong. I'm terrified that without this—" she gestured to the glowing book "—I'll forget how to be brave."

The admission hung in the air between them, honest and vulnerable and exactly the kind of truth-telling she'd learned was necessary for real transformation.

"It's terrifying," she continued, voice growing stronger with each word. "Letting go of the thing that made me feel chosen, special, worthy of adventure. What if without it, I forget what I've learned? What if I slide back into being careful and small and afraid?"

"Then you'll remember again," the Cartographer said simply, voice carrying the weight of wisdom earned through watching countless travelers make this same choice. "Because once you've experienced yourself as brave and growing and capable of wonder, that knowledge doesn't disappear. It might get buried under the ordinary difficulties of daily life, but it doesn't vanish. And remembering becomes easier each time you practice it."

The Cartographer moved closer, its presence somehow both otherworldly and deeply comforting. "Besides, you won't be empty-handed when you return to your ordinary life. You'll have the letter you're going to write to Kit, the notebook you're going to fill with observations and adventures, the memory seed you're going to plant in the soil of your intentions. You'll have the emotional mirror that helps you read the weather of your own heart, and the knowledge that courage is always available to you as a choice rather than a feeling."

Tools. I won't be going back empty-handed. I'll be going back with tools I've learned to use, skills I've developed, perspectives I've earned through experience. The magic won't be gone—it'll just be mine instead of borrowed.

Elsie reached into her pocket and withdrew Sym's emotional mirror, looking at her reflection surrounded by the swirling colors of her inner weather. She could see fear there, yes—purple clouds of uncertainty about giving up the Atlas, grey mists of doubt about her own capacity to maintain the growth she'd experienced. But she could also see golden threads of excitement about the letter she would write, silver sparks of anticipation about Kit's potential response, and underneath it all, a warm, steady glow that she recognized as self-trust earned through experience rather than granted by external validation.

"I see," she said wonderingly. "I can see that I'm afraid, but I can also see that the fear is just information. It's pointing toward what matters most to me—the growth I've experienced, the person I'm becoming, the relationships I want to rebuild. The fear isn't trying to stop me from giving up the Atlas. It's trying to make sure I remember what the Atlas taught me."

As she spoke, something remarkable happened. The Atlas began to change, its pages shifting from the maps of impossible realms to something entirely new. The green leather cover remained the same, but when she looked at the open pages now, she saw not fantastical territories but something far more magical: blank pages, cream-colored and inviting, ready to be filled with whatever story she chose to write.

Her breath caught in her throat, not with fear but with sudden, overwhelming possibility. The transformation felt like watching a butterfly emerge from its cocoon, like seeing the first green shoots of spring push through snow.

"Oh," she breathed, understanding flooding through her with warm certainty. "It's not disappearing. It's transforming."

"The Atlas you found was full of other people's journeys," the Cartographer explained, voice warm with approval and something that might have been pride. "Maps to realms that previous travelers had discovered and explored. But this—" it gestured to the transformed book "—this is yours. A space for you to document your own explorations, both the ones you've completed and the ones yet to come."

Elsie touched the blank pages reverently, feeling their potential pulse under her fingertips. The paper felt warm and welcoming, alive with possibility in the way that all empty pages were alive with the stories they might contain. "I could write about the realms I visited. I could describe the Inch-High Philosophers and Sym and the Memory Orchard. I could create a guide for other people who need to learn that courage is a choice."

"You could," the Cartographer agreed. "Or you could write about the adventures you have in your ordinary life—the magic you create through your choices, the impossible things that become possible when approached with wisdom and wonder and the willingness to risk disappointment in service of growth."

The transformed Atlas felt different in her hands—not heavier or lighter, but somehow more hers. It no longer hummed with the otherworldly energy that had first drawn her to touch its pages, but it pulsed with something far more valuable: the promise of stories yet to be lived, experiences yet to be documented, a life yet to be consciously authored.

This is what trust looks like. Not the absence of fear, but the willingness to act in service of growth even when the outcome is uncertain. The Atlas hasn't been taken from me—I've been given the opportunity to transform it into something that belongs entirely to my own story.

"What about you?" she asked the Cartographer, suddenly aware that this goodbye carried weight she hadn't expected. "What happens to the realms I visited? Do they continue to exist for other travelers?"

"The realms are eternal," the Cartographer replied, its form beginning to shimmer and shift, becoming less defined but somehow more present. "They exist in every moment when someone chooses growth over safety, transformation over stagnation. Every time a person learns to work with their emotions rather than being overwhelmed by them, they visit Sym's realm. Every time someone faces their shadow self with courage rather than avoidance, they walk through the Archive of Inkless Names. Every time someone chooses to author their own story rather than letting fear do the writing, they enter the House of Unfinished Stories."

The understanding settled in her chest like a key turning in a lock. The realms hadn't been separate places she'd visited—they'd been aspects of transformation she'd learned to access and navigate. She would carry them with her always, not as memories but as living capacities.

"You'll carry the realms with you now," the Cartographer continued, voice already growing distant as it prepared to return to whatever space it inhabited between the arrival of travelers who needed its guidance. "Not as places you can escape to, but as territories you can create through your choices. The magic was never separate from you—it was always your own capacity for transformation, waiting to be recognized and claimed."

Around them, The Chair Room began to fade, not disappearing but becoming translucent, as if it were settling back into the realm of possibility from which it had emerged to serve her specific needs. Through the growing transparency, Elsie could see something that made her heart leap with recognition: the familiar interior of her library, but somehow brighter, more alive with potential than she remembered.

Home. Not home as a place to hide from the world, but home as a base of operations for a life lived with intention and courage.

"Are you ready?" the Cartographer asked, voice already growing distant.

Elsie looked around the dissolving Chair Room one last time, at the spiral staircase that had helped her integrate her experiences, at the transformed Atlas that no longer contained other people's maps but waited patiently for her to fill it with her own discoveries. She thought about the letter she would write to Kit, about the notebook she would fill with observations and adventures, about the ordinary Tuesday afternoons that would become magical when lived with attention and intention.

The fear was still there—she could see it in the emotional mirror's reflection, purple clouds of uncertainty about whether she was strong enough to maintain her growth without magical assistance. But alongside the fear was something stronger: a warm, steady glow of self-trust that had been earned through experience rather than granted through external validation.

"Yes," she said, and her voice carried the authority of someone who had learned to trust their own capacity for transformation. "I'm ready to go home. I'm ready to be the author of my own adventure."

The last thing she saw before The Chair Room faded completely was the Cartographer's smile, warm with approval and bright with the promise that real explorers, once they learned to recognize their own courage, never truly lost their way.

And then she was standing in her library, holding a book that looked exactly like the original Atlas but contained infinite blank pages instead of impossible maps, while the late afternoon sunlight painted everything in shades of golden possibility and Minimus adjusted his grip on her shoulder with what might have been satisfaction.

"Well," he said, voice carrying warm contentment, "that was considerably more philosophically complex than I initially anticipated. Shall we see what story you write first?"

Elsie looked around her familiar library—the same books on the same shelves, the same comfortable reading chairs, the same circulation desk where she had spent so many years helping other people find what they were looking for—and realized that everything was exactly the same and completely transformed.

The transformation wasn't in the physical space. It was in her, and therefore in her relationship to everything around her. The books no longer looked like repositories of other people's adventures that she would never be brave enough to live herself. They looked like inspiration, like guides to territories she might explore, like proof that stories were meant to be lived rather than just consumed. The comfortable chairs no longer represented the safety of passive observation. They represented places to rest between adventures, spaces to reflect and plan and gather energy for whatever came next.

"Yes," she said, opening her transformed Atlas to its first blank page and pulling a pen from the cup on her circulation desk. "Let's see what happens when someone decides to become the conscious author of their own life."

She wrote the first words at the top of the page, and they seemed to pulse with their own inner light as her pen moved across the cream-colored paper: *Letter to Kit: On the Nature of Real Explorers and the Art of Finding Each Other Again.*"

Outside, the late afternoon sun painted Maple Street in shades of gold and possibility, and somewhere in Portland, a person who might be Kit looked up from their work with sudden, inexplicable hope, as if they had just felt a story beginning that they had been waiting their whole life to help write.

The magic was real, Elsie understood now. Not because it existed in impossible realms accessible only through enchanted books, but because it lived in every moment when someone chose courage over comfort, growth over safety, the uncertain beauty of attempting over the certain emptiness of not trying.

She began to write, and with each word, the ordinary Tuesday afternoon became a little more magical, and the library around her hummed with the quiet contentment of a space where stories were not just preserved but actively lived.

CHAPTER 9

THE QUIET BETWEEN STORIES

The first thing Elsie noticed about her transformed library was that the silence had changed.

It was still quiet—libraries were supposed to be quiet—but instead of the careful hush of people trying not to disturb anything important, it had become the breathing quiet of a space where stories were actively living. The books seemed to whisper to each other on the shelves, not with desperate loneliness but with satisfied murmur of narratives that knew their purpose.

Or maybe I'm just seeing things differently.

She had returned to work the morning after her journey through the realms, carrying with her the transformed Atlas (which now looked like a perfectly ordinary notebook to anyone else's eyes), Sym's emotional mirror tucked safely in her cardigan pocket, and Minimus, who had taken up residence in a small terrarium she'd created on her desk.

"The ecosystem appears to be thriving," Minimus observed from his carefully arranged habitat of tiny plants and miniature reading chairs. To anyone who happened to notice him, he looked like an unusually iridescent beetle with what might have been a decorative monocle. Only Elsie could hear him speak, and only when she was listening with the part of her that had learned to recognize magic in ordinary moments.

"Everything looks the same," she had said to him on her first morning back, feeling momentarily disoriented by the familiar routine of unlocking doors and switching on lights and brewing tea in the staff room.

"Look again," Minimus had suggested. "With the eyes you've developed rather than the ones you inherited."

So she had looked again, and gradually began to see the differences. They were subtle at first—the way Mrs. Henderson lingered a little longer over the romance novels, as if the books were radiating more invitation than usual. The way the teenage boy who usually rushed through his required reading found himself drawn to the poetry section, running his fingers along spines he'd never noticed before. The way children's storytime seemed to generate more laughter, more wonder, more wide-eyed attention.

But the most significant change was in Elsie herself, and how that internal transformation was rippling outward into every interaction.

Three weeks had passed since her return from the realms, and she was beginning to understand that the magic hadn't stayed in the impossible territories she'd visited. It had followed her home, not as external phenomenon but as a quality of attention, a way of being present that transformed the ordinary into extraordinary simply by recognizing that the distinction had always been artificial.

Though some days I wonder if I imagined the whole thing.

On this particular Tuesday afternoon, she was helping Margaret Winters, a regular patron who came in every week looking for books that might help her cope with her husband's recent death. Margaret was seventy-three, had been married for fifty-one years, and moved through the library with the careful deliberation of someone still learning to navigate a world that no longer made sense.

"I don't know what I'm looking for today," Margaret said, standing in front of the grief and loss section with the defeated posture of someone who had read everything on the subject without finding anything that adequately addressed the specific shape of her loneliness.

Before her journey, Elsie would have offered gentle suggestions, pointed Margaret toward highly rated books about processing grief, perhaps recommended the support group that met in the community room on Thursday evenings. She would have been helpful in the way that librarians were trained to be helpful—competent, resourceful, professionally caring but appropriately distant.

But now, looking at Margaret with eyes that had learned to see emotional weather, Elsie could see something the books about grief didn't address.

She's not just mourning Harold. She's mourning the version of herself that existed in relationship to him. She's lost her identity, not just her partner.

The insight came with such clarity that Elsie had to pause for a moment, checking Sym's emotional mirror discretely to understand what she was sensing. Margaret's emotional pattern showed not just deep blue-black of grief, but swirls of confusion and displacement—the colors of someone who no longer knew how to be herself.

"Margaret," Elsie said, moving from behind the circulation desk to stand beside her patron in the stacks, "can I ask you something a little unconventional?"

Margaret looked surprised but nodded.

Elsie found herself hesitating, thinking of her own experience with loss—not death, but the way she'd mourned the version of herself that had existed in friendship with Kit, the daily rhythms and shared references that had given her life texture before fear convinced her to choose safety over connection.

What would I have needed someone to ask me? What question would have helped me understand that I wasn't just grieving what I'd lost, but struggling to remember who I was when I wasn't defined by that rela-tionship?

"When you and Harold were together, what did you two love to do that you haven't done since he died? Not because it would be too sad, but because it seems too strange to do alone?"

Margaret's eyes filled with tears, but they weren't the helpless tears Elsie had seen her shed before. These were different—tears of recognition rather than despair. Her hand went to her heart, as if something there had just been touched for the first time in months.

"We used to cook together," she said quietly, voice breaking slightly. "Every Sunday, we'd find a new recipe and spend the after-noon making a mess in the kitchen and arguing about whether we'd added too much salt. I haven't cooked anything more complicated than scrambled eggs since the funeral. It feels too..." She paused, searching for the word, face cycling through emotions that seemed to surprise her.

She's remembering what joy felt like. She's remembering that she used to be someone who took pleasure in simple things.

"Too alive?" Elsie suggested gently.

"Yes. Too alive. Like I don't have permission to enjoy things anymore."

Elsie thought about the Memory Orchard, where experiences were preserved not as static recollections but as living things that continued to nourish the people who tended them. She thought about what Mira had taught her about the difference between honoring what was beautiful about the past and imprisoning your-self in it.

What would Mira say? she wondered, then caught herself. *What do I say? What do I know about grief and healing and the courage to keep living fully?*

More than she'd thought, apparently.

"What if we found you some cookbooks?" she said, the sugges-tion emerging from intuition rather than professional training. "Not just any cookbooks, but ones that feel like invitations rather than instructions. Ones that suggest cooking can be a form of conversation, even when you're cooking alone."

She led Margaret through the stacks, but not to the cookbook section. Instead, she found herself drawn to volumes she'd never paid attention to before: memoirs by writers who described food as love language, travel narratives where authors learned to cook local dishes as ways of understanding culture, even a few novels where cooking became a metaphor for the ways people nourish each other across time and distance.

I'm not just finding books. I'm reading the story Margaret is trying to live and helping her find the resources to write the next chapter.

The realization should have felt presumptuous, but instead it felt... right. Natural.

"This one," she said, pulling a book from the shelf almost without conscious thought, "is about a woman who started cooking her way through her grandmother's recipe collection after her grandmother died. Not because she wanted to recreate the past, but because she wanted to continue a conversation that death had interrupted."

Margaret accepted the book with reverence usually reserved for sacred objects. She held it against her chest for a moment, and Elsie could see something shifting in her face—not the resolution of grief, but the beginning of remembering that grief could coexist with other feelings, including hope.

"How did you know?" Margaret asked, looking at Elsie with something that might have been wonder. "That this is exactly what I needed, even though I couldn't articulate it myself?"

Elsie felt a flutter of uncertainty. How could she explain that she'd learned to read emotional weather, that she carried tools gathered in impossible realms, that she'd discovered empathy could be as precise as any other skill when properly developed?

"I think," she said carefully, "I'm learning to listen differently. Not just to what people say they want, but to what they need in order to keep growing."

That's true. And it's true in a way that doesn't require explaining talking beetles or emotion smiths. It's true because I learned to pay attention to the territory of the heart, and that skill works whether I'm in a magical realm or a small-town library.

As Margaret checked out her carefully selected books, her posture had already begun to change. She stood straighter, moved with more purpose, carried herself like someone who had remembered that she was still living a story rather than just cataloging the end of one.

"Thank you," she said to Elsie, and the words carried weight that went beyond gratitude for library services. "I feel like I remember something I'd forgotten."

"What's that?"

Margaret's smile was watery but genuine. "That Harold and I aren't finished talking yet. We're just having the conversation differently now."

After Margaret left, Elsie found herself thinking about the encounter while she reshelfed returns.

This is what the magic looks like in ordinary life. Not dramatic transformations or impossible realms, but moments of recognition where people remember possibilities they'd forgotten existed.

"Impressive demonstration of applied empathy," Minimus observed from his terrarium. "You're developing quite sophisticated emotional sensing capabilities."

"It doesn't feel sophisticated," Elsie said, pausing in her work to consider what had just happened. "It feels like finally paying attention to things I'd been seeing but not noticing for years."

The afternoon brought a steady stream of patrons, each interaction somehow more meaningful than the routine transactions she'd been having for decades. She helped a young mother find picture books that would help explain divorce to her six-year-old, not by recommending standard resources but by intuiting that this particular child needed stories about families that change shape without losing love. She guided a recently retired teacher toward books about second careers, focusing on volumes that treated retirement as transformation rather than diminishment.

Most remarkably, she found herself having a twenty-minute conversation with Jason Chen, a high school senior who usually only came in to use the computers for homework. Today, he seemed restless, distracted, and instead of pretending not to notice his agitation, Elsie found herself asking if he was okay.

"I got accepted to college," he said, as if this were a source of anxiety rather than celebration.

"Congratulations," Elsie said, settling into the chair across from him. "That's wonderful news. Which school?"

"University of Washington. Pre-med program." His voice carried the flat tone of someone reciting information they'd memorized rather than chosen.

He sounds like I used to sound. Like someone who's been told what their life should look like instead of discovering what it could look like.

"And how do you feel about that?"

Jason looked at her with surprise, as if adults didn't usually ask him how he felt about things. His shoulders were tight with tension, and she could see him struggling with whether to give the expected positive response or admit to the uncertainty that was clearly weighing on him.

"I don't know. Scared, I guess. What if I'm not smart enough? What if I hate it? What if I fail out and disappoint everyone who believed in me?"

Elsie thought about The Realm of Scale, where she'd learned that feeling small was often about measuring yourself against the wrong things. She thought about the teenage boy in front of her, overwhelmed by the magnitude of a future that seemed to require him to become someone he wasn't sure he could be.

He's measuring himself against some impossible standard of certainty. Just like I did for decades. He thinks he's supposed to have all the answers instead of being brave enough to live the questions.

She felt herself drawing on lessons from her journey—not

consciously, but the way someone might unconsciously reach for tools they'd learned to use skillfully. The emotional mirror in her pocket warmed slightly, reminding her that uncertainty was information rather than failure.

"Jason," she said gently, leaning forward slightly to match his posture, "can I tell you something that might sound strange?"

He nodded, expression suggesting he was ready for almost anything that might provide relief from the pressure he was carrying.

What would have helped me at his age? What would have changed everything if someone had told me that not knowing was acceptable, even necessary?

"The most important question isn't whether you're smart enough or brave enough or anything else enough. The most important question is whether you're curious enough to keep learning, flexible enough to change course when you discover new information about yourself, and kind enough to forgive yourself for being human while you figure it out."

Jason stared at her for a long moment, expression cycling through surprise, relief, and something that looked like hope. "That's not what anyone else has told me."

"What has everyone else told you?"

"That I have to know what I want, have to be committed, have to work harder than everyone else if I want to succeed. That there's no room for uncertainty or mistakes."

The same messages I internalized. The same impossible standards that convinced me I wasn't allowed to be anything less than perfect.

She thought about her own journey, about all the years she'd spent trying to be perfect instead of trying to be honest, all the opportunities she'd missed because she was afraid of not being good enough rather than curious about what she might discover if she tried.

"What if," she said, voice warming with conviction, "the point isn't to have all the answers, but to be brave enough to live the questions? What if uncertainty isn't a problem to be solved, but information to help you navigate more wisely?"

She watched Jason's posture change as he considered this, shoulders relaxing slightly as if he'd been given permission to not have everything figured out. The tight lines around his eyes softened, and for the first time since she'd known him, he looked his actual age rather than like someone trying to be older and more certain than any teenager should have to be.

"You really think that's okay?" he asked, voice carrying vulnerable honesty of someone testing a new possibility. "Not knowing exactly what I want or who I'm supposed to become?"

"I think," Elsie said, drawing on everything she'd learned about the difference between wisdom and knowing, "that the people who pretend to have everything figured out are usually the ones who've stopped paying attention to their own growth. I think uncertainty can be a compass if you learn to read it properly."

I spent thirty years being afraid of not knowing, and it took a journey through impossible realms to teach me that not knowing is just the beginning of discovery.

She found herself recommending books she'd never paid attention to before—volumes about finding direction through exploration rather than predetermined destinations, memoirs by people who'd changed careers multiple times and discovered that each transition had taught them something valuable about their own capacity for reinvention.

As Jason gathered his selections and prepared to leave, he paused at the circulation desk. "Ms. Vine," he said, voice carrying genuine curiosity, "you seem different lately. I mean, you were always nice, but now you seem more... present, I guess. Like you're really seeing people instead of just helping them find books."

Elsie felt a warm glow that had nothing to do with professional satisfaction and everything to do with recognition that her internal changes were creating ripples in ways she hadn't fully anticipated.

He sees it too. The transformation isn't just internal—it's changing how I move through the world, how I connect with people, how I understand what help actually means.

"Thank you for noticing," she said. "I think I'm learning to pay better attention to the stories people are living instead of just the books they're looking for."

After the library closed, Elsie sat at her desk with her transformed Atlas open to a fresh page, documenting the day's encounters with the same careful attention she had once reserved for cataloging new acquisitions. But instead of recording titles and authors and Dewey Decimal classifications, she was mapping the territory of human connection, documenting moments when ordinary interactions became opportunities for recognition and growth.

Margaret Winters, she wrote, *rediscovering that love continues conversation across the boundaries of death through the medium of Sunday afternoon cooking projects.*

Jason Chen, learning that uncertainty can be a compass rather than a failure to navigate properly.

The unnamed teenager who spent twenty minutes in the poetry section, reading aloud in whispers, practicing the sound of words that might help him understand what he's feeling.

Mrs. Henderson, who checked out three romance novels and a book about traveling alone, suggesting internal adventures are beginning to coordinate with external possibilities.

As she wrote, Minimus observed from his terrarium with what might have been approval. "You're becoming quite the anthropologist of transformation," he noted. "Documenting the daily magic of people discovering they're more capable of growth than they previously suspected."

"Is that what I'm doing?" Elsie asked, pausing in her writing to consider the day's patterns.

"Among other things. You're also demonstrating that magic doesn't require impossible realms—it simply requires the willingness to see extraordinary potential that exists in ordinary moments when approached with attention and intention."

Elsie looked around her library, seeing it with eyes that had learned to recognize magic in the most mundane circumstances. The books on their shelves weren't just repositories of other people's stories—they were invitations to transformation, doorways to territories of the heart that anyone could explore if they learned to read not just with their eyes but with their capacity for recognition and wonder.

The comfortable chairs weren't just furniture—they were spaces where people could rest between discoveries, places to process new insights and gather energy for whatever growth came next. The circulation desk wasn't just a workspace—it was a compass point where people could find not just books but guidance toward unexplored territories of their own possibilities.

Most remarkably, the quiet between stories had become a living thing, a breathing space where transformation could occur not through dramatic revelation but through patient accumulation of moments where people remembered they were more than they had previously imagined.

As she locked up the library and walked home through familiar streets of Millbrook, Elsie carried with her the satisfaction of someone who had discovered that the most important adventures didn't require departure from ordinary life—they required the courage to live ordinary life with extraordinary attention.

In her pocket, the memory seed Mira had given her pulsed gently with warmth of intentions being watered by daily acts of conscious choice, growing into experiences that would surprise and delight the person who chose to tend them with care.

The alchemy was amazing, more real than it had ever been when confined to impossible realms accessed through enchanted books. It lived in every moment when someone chose growth over stagnation, connection over isolation, the uncertain beauty of attempting over the certain emptiness of not trying.

And tomorrow, she would return to her library, carrying with her the knowledge that she was not just a curator of other people's stories but an active participant in the daily magic of helping people discover they were the authors of adventures worth documenting.

The extraordinary had been hiding in the ordinary all along, waiting for someone brave enough to recognize it and skilled enough to help others claim it for themselves.

CHAPTER 10

THE DOOR THAT DOESN'T CLOSE

The first echo appeared on a Thursday morning in the form of Dr. Eugene Threadworth, professor emeritus of philosophy at the state university, who arrived at the Millbrook Public Library carrying a briefcase that seemed entirely too small for his towering frame and a notebook filled with what appeared to be elaborate debates about the fundamental nature of existence.

Elsie looked up from processing new acquisitions to find him standing at her desk, peering at her through wire-rimmed glasses with the intense scrutiny of someone who had spent decades contemplating questions that had no definitive answers.

"Excuse me," he said in a voice that carried the particular cadence of academic discourse, "but I'm looking for reading material that addresses the philosophical implications of scale. Specifically, whether significance is an inherent property of an object or event, or whether it's determined by the perspective of the observer."

Elsie's pen froze over the catalog card she'd been filling out. The question was so precisely aligned with the lessons she'd learned in The Realm of Scale that she might have suspected Dr. Threadworth of having witnessed her conversations with the Inch-High Philosophers, except that he was entirely normal-sized and showed no signs of having recently debated dust-mote intellectuals.

This can't be coincidence. He's asking exactly the questions the philosophers taught me to explore. He's wrestling with the same insights about how significance depends on what you measure against.

Or maybe she was reading too much into it. Maybe she was so changed by her experiences that she was seeing connections everywhere.

"That's... a very specific inquiry," she said, studying his face for any indication that he might be more than he appeared.

"Indeed. I've recently found myself preoccupied with the notion that our understanding of what matters may be entirely dependent on what we choose to measure it against." He adjusted his glasses with the precise gesture of someone who treated even minor actions as subjects worthy of philosophical consideration. "For instance, is a dust mote insignificant because it's small, or is our perception of its insignificance merely a function of our own limited perspective?"

From his terrarium, Minimus's antennae twitched with what Elsie had learned to recognize as amusement. "Fascinating," he whispered, just loudly enough for her to hear. "It appears your journey has created resonances that extend beyond your own consciousness."

The realms are echoing. Dr. Threadworth isn't just someone who happens to be interested in scale—he's carrying the wisdom I learned from the Inch-High Philosophers, processing it through his own intellectual framework.

But even as the thought formed, doubt crept in. *Or I'm just noticing these conversations because I'm paying attention differently now. Maybe these philosophical discussions were always happening, and I was too self-absorbed to notice.*

Elsie led Dr. Threadworth to the philosophy section, but found herself drawn to books she'd never noticed before—volumes that addressed the relationship between perspective and meaning, treatises on the nature of significance, essays that explored whether importance was discovered or created through the act of attention.

I know what he needs. Not because I've read these books, but because I've lived the questions they explore.

"This one might interest you," she said, pulling a slim volume from the shelf. "It's about how meaning emerges from the interaction between observer and observed, rather than existing independently in either."

Dr. Threadworth accepted the book with reverence usually reserved for sacred texts. "Precisely what I was hoping to find, though I couldn't have articulated it so clearly myself." He paused, studying her with the intensity of someone encountering an unexpected phenomenon. "You have a remarkable intuition for philosophical inquiry. Have you studied the subject formally?"

"Not exactly," Elsie said, thinking of tiny philosophers with dandelion-fluff beards who had taught her that size was always relative to context. "But I've had some... experiential education in questions of scale and significance."

As Dr. Threadworth settled into one of the reading chairs with his selected volumes, Elsie couldn't shake the feeling that she was witnessing something more than coincidence. The way he held himself, the precise cadence of his speech, even his intense focus on questions that most people would consider abstract—everything about him echoed the essence of the Inch-High Philosophers.

But maybe that's just what philosophers are like, she thought, trying to ground herself. *Maybe I'm seeing magical connections where there are just intellectual ones.*

"Is he real?" she whispered to Minimus when she returned to her desk.

"Define real," Minimus replied unhelpfully. "He appears to possess corporeal form and genuine intellectual curiosity. Whether he exists independently of your journey or represents some form of dimensional overflow from the realms is perhaps less important than the fact that he's found exactly the resources he needs."

The afternoon brought more echoes, each one subtly different but unmistakably connected to the territories she had explored. A young woman named Sophia arrived asking for books about emotional regulation, but not in the clinical psychology sense—she wanted to understand how feelings could be transformed into tools for conscious living rather than simply managed or suppressed.

"I've been having the strangest dreams," Sophia explained as Elsie helped her navigate resources on emotional intelligence and mindful awareness. "Dreams about places where the landscape changes based on what you're feeling, where anger builds bridges and sadness creates rivers and joy causes flowers to bloom spontaneously. It sounds crazy when I say it out loud."

She's dreaming of Sym's realm. She's processing the same lessons about emotions being tools rather than weather. The realm is reaching her through dreams because she's ready for that understanding.

Or maybe, the more rational part of her mind suggested, Sophia was just someone who intuitively understood emotional intelligence and was expressing it in metaphorical terms.

"It doesn't sound crazy at all," Elsie assured her, thinking of Sym and the realm where reality responded to emotional states. "It sounds like wisdom trying to teach you something important about the relationship between inner weather and external experience."

She found herself recommending books she'd never read but somehow knew would be perfect: volumes about treating emotions as information rather than intrusion, guides to using feelings as compasses for navigation rather than storms to be weathered.

I can see what she needs. Not just any books about emotions, but ones that will help her understand what Sym taught me—that feelings are tools for conscious living when you learn to work with them instead of being overwhelmed by them.

"How did you know?" Sophia asked as she checked out her selections. "These are exactly what I need, even though I couldn't have explained what I was looking for."

"I think," Elsie said, "sometimes the books we need find us through the people who've learned to listen to the same lessons we're ready to hear."

Or I'm just getting better at reading people, she added silently. *Maybe this is what happens when you pay attention to emotional patterns instead of just surface requests.*

Later that day, an elderly gentleman named Marcus Rivera arrived with a request that made Elsie's heart skip: he wanted materials about memory preservation, but specifically about the difference between honoring the past and being imprisoned by it.

"My wife passed away two years ago," he explained, settling into the chair across from Elsie's desk with careful movements. "Everyone tells me I need to 'move on,' but that feels like betrayal. At the same time, I know Eleanor wouldn't want me to stop living because she's not here anymore."

The Memory Orchard. He's struggling with exactly what Mira taught me—the difference between preserving experiences as living things that nourish growth versus trapping yourself in static recollections that prevent change.

"What if," she suggested gently, "the choice isn't between moving on or staying stuck? What if there's a third option—growing forward while carrying the best parts of what you shared with you?"

Marcus's eyes lit up with recognition, as if she had named something he'd been feeling but couldn't articulate. "Yes. Exactly. Like... like the love becomes part of who you are, but it helps you become more rather than keeping you frozen."

He understands immediately. He was already almost there—he just needed someone to give him permission to trust his own instincts about how love works.

The books Elsie found for him weren't in the grief and loss section. They were scattered throughout the library: a memoir about a gardener who planted new varieties in honor of his deceased partner, a collection of essays about how gratitude for shared experiences could fuel new adventures, a novel about a widow who learned to cook her way through her late husband's travel journal.

"You've given me something I didn't know I was looking for," Marcus said as he prepared to leave, his posture already straighter, more purposeful. "The permission to love Eleanor more by living more, rather than loving her more by living less."

That's exactly what Mira would say. Memory as nourishment for future growth, not chains that prevent it.

As the pattern of echoes continued over the following days, Elsie began to understand what was happening. The realms hadn't vanished when she'd given up the Atlas—they had integrated into the ordinary world, manifesting not as places she could visit but as wisdom that could appear wherever it was needed.

The magic is leaking through. Or maybe it was always here, and I just learned to recognize it. Maybe transformation creates space for more transformation, like ripples spreading outward from a stone dropped in still water.

Or maybe, the skeptical voice in her head suggested, she was just noticing patterns that had always been there because her experiences had taught her to pay attention differently.

Does it matter which explanation is true? she wondered. *The effect is the same—people are getting exactly the help they need.*

Dr. Threadworth returned daily, engaging other patrons in philosophical discussions that would have seemed impossibly abstract except that they somehow addressed exactly the existential questions people were wrestling with. His presence turned the library into an informal philosophy salon, where conversations about the nature of significance helped a struggling graduate student realize that her research mattered even if it never made headlines.

Sophia became a regular fixture as well, drawn not just to the emotional intelligence section but to poetry and art books and travel narratives. She started an informal discussion group for other patrons interested in emotional literacy, meeting every Tuesday evening in the community room.

Marcus discovered that the library had become a place where his memories of Eleanor felt particularly alive and welcome. He began volunteering to help with local history projects, finding that his skill at preserving and honoring the past without being trapped by it made him uniquely qualified to help other community members research their family histories.

But the most remarkable echo was the one that appeared on a rainy Wednesday afternoon in the form of a letter.

Elsie was processing returns when Mrs. Henderson approached her desk carrying a small envelope with an expression of bemused curiosity.

"This came for you in today's mail delivery," she said, "but it's addressed rather strangely. Instead of your name, it just says 'The Librarian Who Remembers How to Dream.' The postal worker said it had been forwarded from Portland, through several bookstores, and somehow ended up here."

Elsie's hands trembled as she accepted the envelope. The handwriting was unfamiliar yet somehow completely recognizable, flowing and confident with the particular ink stains that suggested someone who still preferred fountain pens despite their impracticality.

Kit. It has to be Kit. No one else would address a letter that way, no one else would understand that I've become someone who remembers how to dream.

Inside, written on paper that smelled faintly of cedar and coffee and the particular scent of someone who spent their days surrounded by books and maps, was a single page:

Dear Fellow Explorer,

I don't know your name, but I know your story. Or at least, I know the version of it that's been haunting my dreams since I received a letter addressed to bookstores in Portland, asking them to forward it to someone named Kit who might remember making promises about impossible expeditions and never forgetting how to dream big.

I am that Kit. Or rather, I am a Kit—Kris Thorne, owner of Atlas Books and Curiosities, a shop that specializes in travel literature, maps to places that may or may not exist, and books that seem to find their way to exactly the people who need them. I have ink-stained fingers and an unshakeable belief in the possibility of impossible things and a very clear memory of a childhood friend who shared my conviction that the world was far more magical than most people suspected.

I also have a box of letters I never sent, addressed to someone whose face I can remember perfectly but whose last name escaped me decades ago. Letters filled with descriptions of the adventures I've had and the places I've discovered and the growing certainty that some promises transcend the ordinary limitations of time and distance and the question of whether we can find each other again.

Your letter reached me at exactly the moment when I most needed to remember that some stories don't end just because life becomes complicated. That some friendships exist in the spaces between memory and possibility, waiting patiently for the right conditions to manifest in ordinary reality.

I'm writing this on a Tuesday afternoon, sitting in my bookstore surrounded by maps and travel guides and the accumulated evidence of a life spent seeking out the magical and mysterious. Outside my window, Portland is doing its best impression of a city that takes itself seriously, but I keep catching glimpses of impossible territories in the reflections of rain-soaked streets, hearing echoes of conversations we had when we were young and certain that everywhere was worth exploring.

I don't know if you're the Elsie I remember, or if you're someone else entirely who happened to need the same lessons about courage and transformation and the willingness to author your own adventure. But I know this: real explorers always find each other, and I've been waiting forty-five years for someone brave enough to send the first signal.

So here's my response: I remember. I remember planning expeditions to impossible places and making promises about never forgetting how to dream big and saying goodbye with the absolute conviction that our paths would cross again when we were ready for the real adventure to begin.

I think we might be ready now.

If you're willing to risk the disappointment of discovering that I'm not quite the person you remember, or the joy of finding out that some friendships only get better when given thirty years to mature, I'll be in Millbrook next Saturday afternoon. I'll be the one sitting in the library, surrounded by maps and notebooks and the accumulated evidence of a life spent believing in impossible things, waiting to see if the girl who promised to fill a compass rose notebook with adventures has finally found stories worth documenting.

Your fellow cartographer of the impossible, Kit

P.S. - I still have my grandfather's compass. It points not to magnetic north, but to the place where wonder lives in the ordinary world. It's been pointing toward Millbrook for weeks now.

Elsie read the letter three times, her heart racing with a mixture of joy and terror and the particular excitement that comes from realizing that some stories write themselves toward exactly the ending they were always meant to have.

They remember. They remember the promises, the dreams, the conviction that real explorers always find each other. And they've been carrying letters they never sent, just like I've been carrying words I never wrote.

But alongside the joy came a flutter of panic. *What if I'm disappointing in person? What if thirty years of careful living has made me too small for someone who's spent their life seeking out the magical and mysterious?*

The letter felt warm in her hands, as if it carried not just ink and paper but some essential quality of the person who had written it. She could almost see Kit in their bookstore, surrounded by maps and possibility, writing with the same intensity they'd brought to childhood planning sessions.

Atlas Books and Curiosities. Of course they would own a bookstore that specializes in maps to places that may or may not exist. Of course they would have built a life that kept wonder alive in the ordinary world.

"Good news?" Mrs. Henderson asked, noticing her expression.

"The best kind," Elsie said, folding the letter carefully and slipping it into her pocket beside Sym's emotional mirror and the memory seed that had been growing stronger with each passing day. "The kind that requires courage to fully appreciate."

Saturday. Four days to prepare for the possibility that some promises can actually be kept, that some friendships can survive decades of silence and the accumulated caution that comes with learning how much it's possible to lose.

She looked around her library, seeing it with new eyes: not just as the place where she worked, but as the space where she had learned to recognize magic in ordinary moments. The place where echoes from impossible realms had found ways to manifest as wisdom available to anyone willing to pay attention.

This is where Kit will find me. Not in some impossible realm, but here, in the place where I learned that ordinary life could be magical when lived with attention and intention. Surrounded by books and the quiet hum of stories being discovered by people who need them.

"Minimus," she whispered, "I think our story is about to get significantly more interesting."

"Indeed," he replied, adjusting his tiny monocle with satisfaction. "I do so enjoy witnessing the moment when potential crystallizes into actuality. Saturday should prove quite educational."

Outside, the rain continued to fall on Millbrook's familiar streets, but in the reflection of water-streaked windows, Elsie could swear she saw the outline of impossible territories waiting to be explored by two middle-aged adventurers who had finally learned that the most important maps were the ones that led not to places, but to each other.

The door between her journey and her ordinary life hadn't closed when she'd given up the Atlas. Instead, it had become a permanent opening, allowing magic to flow from the impossible realms into the daily world, and wisdom gained through extraordinary experience to transform ordinary moments into opportunities for wonder.

Saturday was four days away. She had a notebook to finish filling and a response to write and the delicate work of preparing her heart for the possibility that some promises, despite decades of silence, could still be kept by people brave enough to risk the beautiful uncertainty of beginning again.

The story isn't ending. It's just beginning. All of this—the realms, the tools, the integration—it was preparation for whatever comes next.

The transformation was complete, but the adventure was just beginning.

CHAPTER 11

KIT AND THE INK THAT STAYS

Saturday arrived with the kind of golden October light that made even ordinary moments feel touched by magic, and Elsie woke with the particular mixture of anticipation and terror that comes from knowing your life is about to change in ways you can't predict or control.

She had spent the week in careful preparation that felt more like tending to a ritual than simply getting ready to meet an old friend. She'd filled the remaining pages of Kit's compass rose notebook with descriptions of her journey through the realms. But she also added observations about the daily magic she'd learned to recognize—the way Tuesday afternoons could become adventures when approached with attention, how helping library patrons find exactly what they needed felt like a form of cartography.

She'd written and rewritten her response to Kit's letter seventeen times before settling on a version that managed to convey both her joy at the reconnection and her honest anxiety about whether thirty years of separate growth had made them too different to reclaim what they'd shared as children.

What if we have nothing to talk about? What if the magic I felt

146

reading their letter doesn't translate into actual connection when we're sitting in the same room?

She'd even consulted Sym's emotional mirror repeatedly, watching the swirling colors of her internal weather shift between golden excitement and purple uncertainty, learning to read her own anticipation not as a problem to be solved but as information about how much this meeting mattered to her.

Now, standing in front of her bathroom mirror at seven in the morning, she found herself wondering who she was dressing for. The Kit she remembered from childhood? The Christopher Thorne who owned a bookstore in Portland? Or the person she hoped to become through showing up authentically for whatever this reunion might bring?

All of the above, she decided, settling on clothes that felt both comfortable and intentional—a soft sweater the color of forest shadows, her most flattering jeans, and boots that looked capable of walking interesting distances. She wanted to look like someone who had learned to take up appropriate space in the world.

"Nervous?" Minimus asked from his terrarium as she prepared to leave for the library, where she would spend the morning trying to work normally while actually counting down hours until Kit's promised arrival.

"Terrified," Elsie admitted. "What if we don't recognize each other? What if the people we've become have nothing in common beyond shared nostalgia?"

"And what if it does?" Minimus countered gently. "What if thirty years of parallel growth has made you more compatible rather than less? What if the courage you've developed makes you better prepared for meaningful friendship than you were as children?"

Elsie considered this as she made her morning tea, thinking about how much she'd changed during her journey through the realms and in the weeks since. The woman who had first touched the Atlas's pages had been so afraid of disappointment that she'd rarely risked hoping for anything beyond safety. The woman in her kitchen now had learned to treat uncertainty as information rather than threat.

I suppose the question isn't whether we'll still be compatible. The question is whether I'm brave enough to find out.

The morning at the library passed with agonizing slowness despite her best efforts to lose herself in routine tasks. She processed returns, helped patrons, and engaged in meaningful conversations that had become her new normal, but part of her attention remained fixed on the clock, watching minutes tick toward two o'clock with the intensity of someone awaiting a verdict.

Dr. Threadworth arrived for his daily philosophical consultation, this time bringing a question about temporal experience that felt suspiciously relevant to her situation.

"I've been pondering," he said, settling into his usual reading chair, "whether it's possible for two people to maintain a meaningful connection across decades of separation, or whether the passage of time inevitably transforms us so completely that reunion becomes a meeting between strangers who happen to share a history."

Is he actually asking about his own situation, or does he somehow know about mine?

"What do you think?" Elsie asked, though she suspected his inquiry wasn't entirely theoretical.

"I think the answer depends on whether the connection was based on circumstance or on recognition. Circumstantial friendships —those built on shared experiences or temporary proximity—rarely survive significant separation. But relationships based on recognition of something essential in the other person, something that exists beneath surface changes, those connections can transcend both time and transformation."

"And how do you tell the difference?"

Dr. Threadworth smiled with the satisfaction of someone who had arrived at a particularly elegant conclusion. "By paying attention to whether your memory of the person focuses on what you did together or on who you discovered yourself to be in their presence.

External experiences fade and change meaning over time, but the way someone helps you understand yourself—that recognition tends to remain constant even as both parties continue to grow."

Elsie thought about her memories of Kit, realizing that what she remembered most clearly wasn't specific adventures they'd planned or particular books they'd read together, but the way Kit's absolute conviction that impossible things were worth pursuing had helped her believe she was someone capable of extraordinary experiences.

That's exactly what I needed to hear.

"Thank you," she said. "That's... remarkably helpful perspective."

"Philosophy is most valuable when it addresses the questions we're actually living rather than the ones we think we should be contemplating."

At one-thirty, Elsie found herself unable to concentrate on anything resembling work. She kept glancing toward the library's front entrance, watching for a figure that might match her mental image of how Kit would look after three decades.

At one forty-five, she gave up all pretense of productivity and positioned herself at the circulation desk with a clear view of the door, her transformed Atlas open to a fresh page where she planned to document whatever happened next, regardless of whether it turned out to be beautiful or disappointing.

At exactly two o'clock, the door opened.

The person who entered looked like Kit and nothing like Kit and exactly like Kit all at the same time. Taller than she'd expected, with silver threading through hair that still refused to cooperate, wearing clothes that managed to look both practical and adventurous. The ink stains on their fingers were exactly as she remembered, and they carried a leather messenger bag that bulged with notebooks and maps.

But it was the eyes that convinced her—creek-water gray-green eyes that lit up with recognition and joy and something that might have been relief as they scanned the library and settled on her face.

"Elsie," Kit said, and their voice carried thirty years of changes but still held the warm certainty that had made impossible things seem achievable.

"Kit," she replied, and found that she was crying without having decided to, tears of recognition and gratitude and the particular joy that comes from discovering that some connections transcend ordinary limitations.

They stood looking at each other across the library's main floor for a moment that felt both eternal and instantaneous, taking in evidence of who they'd each become while searching for confirmation of who they'd always been.

Then Kit was moving toward her, and she was coming around the circulation desk, and they were embracing with fierce intensity of people who had thought they might never have the chance again.

"You're real," Elsie said into Kit's shoulder, breathing in scent that was both completely unfamiliar and somehow exactly right—coffee and cedar and ink and the particular smell of someone who spent time surrounded by books and possibilities.

"You're real," Kit replied, voice carrying wonder and satisfaction in equal measure. "And you're exactly who I hoped you'd become."

The familiar scent of lemon oil from the morning's shelf cleaning seemed to intensify around them, as if the library itself was witnessing this moment, blessing their reunion with the comforting smell of well-tended books and carefully maintained wood.

They separated enough to look at each other properly, hands still resting on each other's arms as if to maintain proof of physical presence.

"You look..." Elsie began, then paused, searching for adequate words.

"Older?" Kit suggested with a smile that held all the mischief she remembered. "More weathered? Distinguished by decades of questionable decision-making?"

"You look like someone who kept all the promises we made," Elsie said, and Kit's expression shifted into something softer, more vulnerable.

"Not all of them," Kit admitted. "But I kept the important ones. I kept believing in impossible things. I kept looking for magic in ordinary places. I kept the conviction that some adventures are worth waiting for, even when the waiting stretches longer than expected."

"I broke my promises," Elsie said, the confession emerging before she could edit it. "I let fear make me small. I chose safety over possibility so many times that I forgot possibility even existed."

Kit's hands moved to frame her face, touch gentle but firm. "But you remembered," they said with the kind of certainty that made doubt seem foolish. "You remembered, and you did something about it, and you wrote a letter brave enough to travel across time and space to find me. That's not breaking promises—that's keeping them in the only way that ultimately matters."

They talked for hours. Not just talked—they shared stories with the intensity of people who had thirty years of experiences to exchange and the precious gift of an audience who understood the significance of details that might seem irrelevant to anyone else.

Kit told her about the bookstore they'd built in Portland, about how it had become a gathering place for people who needed to believe in magic but weren't sure where to look for it. They described customers who arrived looking for practical travel guides and left with books about internal landscapes, people who came seeking maps to specific destinations and discovered atlases to territories of the heart.

"It turns out," Kit said, settling into the comfortable reading chair Elsie had positioned beside her desk, "that everyone is looking for the same thing we were looking for as children—proof that the world is more magical than it appears, and permission to be the kind of person who goes looking for that magic."

Elsie described her journey through the realms, watching Kit's eyes grow bright with recognition and delight as she detailed her encounters with the Inch-High Philosophers, her lessons from Sym about emotions as tools, her experience in the Memory Orchard.

"You found it," Kit said when she'd finished, voice carrying awe and something that might have been pride. "You found the doorway we always knew was hidden somewhere. You became the explorer we always planned to be."

"We both did," Elsie corrected. "Just through different territories."

Kit reached into their messenger bag and withdrew a notebook—not unlike the one they'd given her decades ago, but this one filled with years of entries. They opened it to a random page and began reading:

"Tuesday, March 15th. Helped a woman find a guidebook to Scotland, but what she really needed was permission to travel alone after her husband's death. Ended up giving her three memoirs about solo adventures that started as healing journeys. She left looking ten years younger and infinitely more possible."

"You've been documenting the same magic I've been learning to recognize," Elsie said wonderingly. "The way ordinary moments become extraordinary when approached with the right mixture of attention and intention."

"I think we've been living parallel adventures without realizing it. You learned to navigate impossible realms that helped you understand your own heart. I learned to recognize magic in daily life that helped other people understand theirs. But we were both doing the same work—learning that courage is a choice, that wonder is available to anyone willing to look for it."

The afternoon light was fading when Kit finally asked the question that had been hovering between them.

"So what happens now?" they said. "We're forty-five instead of sixteen, with lives and responsibilities and decades of accumulated habits. We can't just run away and become full-time explorers of the impossible, much as that might appeal to our inner twelve-year-olds."

That's the practical question I've been avoiding thinking about.

Elsie thought about this, looking around her library where

echoes from the realms had been appearing with increasing frequency, where her work had become a form of daily magic.

"What if we don't have to choose between responsibility and adventure? What if the real exploration is learning to live our regular lives with enough consciousness and intention that they become the adventures we always planned to have?"

Kit's face lit up with the same expression she remembered from childhood moments when they'd solved a particularly complex puzzle. "You mean like... collaborative cartography? Mapping the territories of conscious living from two different base camps, sharing discoveries, planning expeditions that might involve visiting each other but don't require abandoning the work we're already doing?"

"Exactly. You keep helping people find magic in Portland. I keep helping people discover their own capacity for transformation in Millbrook. We write letters about what we're learning, plan visits that feel like expeditions, share resources and insights."

"Correspondence adventures," Kit said with growing enthusiasm. "Documentation of the daily magic. Collaborative exploration of what it means to be adults who never forgot how to believe in impossible things."

They spent the next hour making plans with the same detailed enthusiasm they'd brought to childhood schemes, but now backed by decades of practical experience and hard-won wisdom about what kinds of adventures were actually sustainable for people with jobs and responsibilities.

They would write weekly letters documenting discoveries and sharing resources. Kit would create a section in their bookstore dedicated to "Practical Magic"—books that helped people recognize wonder in ordinary circumstances. Elsie would start a monthly program at the library for people interested in "Applied Wonder."

Most importantly, they would visit each other regularly, treating these reunions not as breaks from real life but as intensive workshops in collaborative exploration.

As they prepared to part—Kit needed to drive back to Portland that evening, but had promised to return the following weekend—Elsie pulled out her transformed Atlas and opened it to the page where she'd been documenting the day's events.

"Would you write something? Something to commemorate this reunion, to mark the beginning of whatever story we're going to write together from here?"

Kit accepted the pen and considered for a moment before writing:

"October 15th. Elsie Vine and Christopher Thorne, forty-five-year-old explorers of the possible, officially resumed the expedition that began thirty years ago when two children decided that the world was far more magical than most people suspected. Current mission: proving that the most important adventures happen not in distant territories but in the conscious choice to live ordinary life with extraordinary attention. Status: Ready to begin."

Below that, they drew a compass rose identical to the one that had decorated the notebook they'd given her decades ago, but this one pointing not to magnetic north but to a destination labeled simply: "Wonder."

"Perfect," Elsie said, watching the ink dry on a page that felt like the beginning of a story she'd been waiting her entire life to live.

As Kit prepared to leave, they paused at the library door and looked back with profound satisfaction.

"You know what I realized today?"

"What?"

"We did it. We actually did it. We became the explorers we always planned to be. Not in the way we expected when we were children, but in the way that actually matters—we learned to recognize magic, to live consciously, to choose wonder over safety. We became adults who kept the promises our twelve-year-old selves made about never forgetting how to dream big."

After Kit left, Elsie sat alone in her library as the autumn evening painted everything in shades of gold and possibility. Around her, the space hummed with quiet contentment of a place where stories lived and grew and found their way to exactly the people who needed them.

From his terrarium, Minimus observed her with what might have been satisfaction. "Well," he said, adjusting his tiny monocle, "that appeared to unfold remarkably well. Are you pleased with how the story turned out?"

"It's not turned out," Elsie said, closing her Atlas on a page that felt like a beginning rather than an ending. "It's just turned toward. We're finally ready to write the story we've been preparing for our entire lives."

She looked around her familiar library, seeing it with eyes that had learned to recognize magic in the most ordinary circumstances. Tomorrow, she would return to her regular work of helping people find exactly what they needed, but now that work would be informed by the knowledge that she was not just a librarian but a cartographer of possibility, not just a curator of other people's stories but an active author of adventures worth documenting.

The door between transformation and daily life would never close again, because she had learned that there had never been a door at all—only the artificial boundary between who she had thought she was and who she had always been capable of becoming.

Outside, the October evening settled over Millbrook with the particular quality of light that makes even familiar streets look like territories waiting to be explored by people brave enough to approach them with attention and intention and the unshakeable conviction that magic is always available to those who remember how to look for it.

The adventure was just beginning.

CHAPTER 12

THE LIBRARIAN'S ANSWER

Three months after Kit's first visit to Millbrook, Elsie stood before a gathering of forty-seven people in the Millbrook Public Library's main reading room, holding in her hands the transformed Atlas that had become both the record of her journey and the invitation for others to begin their own explorations of the possible.

Forty-seven people. Jesus. I was expecting maybe twelve.

The faces looking back at her represented a cross-section of her community that would have seemed impossible to assemble before her transformation: Dr. Threadworth sat in the front row beside Sophia, who had become the library's unofficial coordinator for emotional literacy programs. Marcus Rivera had brought three other widowed friends who were interested in learning how to honor the past while remaining open to future possibilities. Jason Chen sat with his mother, both of them curious about what the librarian who had helped him reframe uncertainty as a compass might have to share about conscious living.

Mrs. Henderson occupied her usual spot near the biography section, flanked by two members of the book club she'd convinced to read memoirs by people who had completely transformed their lives after age fifty. Near the back, she could see several teenagers who had been drawn by word-of-mouth reports that Ms. Vine had somehow become the kind of adult who talked about emotions and dreams without being either condescending or impractical.

Most remarkably, Kit sat in the second row, having arrived that morning for what had become a monthly pilgrimage to Millbrook, their notebook open and ready to document whatever insights emerged from this experiment in public vulnerability.

Okay, Elsie. Don't overthink this. Just tell them the truth.

"I want to tell you a story," Elsie began, her voice carrying the quiet confidence of someone who had learned to trust both her own experience and her audience's capacity for wonder. "It's the story of a librarian who spent twenty-three years helping other people find what they were looking for while never quite knowing what she was looking for herself."

She opened her Atlas to the first entry she'd written upon her return from the realms, but instead of reading it directly, she looked up at her audience with an expression of gentle invitation.

"Before I begin, I want you to know that everything I'm going to share with you is true. But it's true in the way that fairy tales are true—not because every detail corresponds to what we usually call reality, but because it points toward truths about transformation and courage and the human capacity for growth. Things that are more real than most of the facts we memorize."

Please let them understand what I mean by that. Please let them not think I've completely lost my mind.

Dr. Threadworth nodded approvingly, while several of the teenagers leaned forward with the particular intensity that suggested they were hungry for exactly this kind of truth-telling.

Elsie began to read, not from her Atlas directly, but from memory that had been refined and clarified by months of documenting the daily magic she'd learned to recognize. She told them about discovering a book that shouldn't exist, about the choice between chairs that offered safety and doors that promised transformation. She described realms where thoughts became geography, where emotions shaped reality, where memories grew like fruit on impossible trees.

But more importantly, she told them about what those impossible experiences had taught her about the possible ones available in ordinary life.

"The Realm of Scale," she said, "taught me that feeling small is usually about measuring yourself against the wrong things. I met philosophers the size of dust motes who spoke about existence and meaning with complete authority, and I realized that significance isn't about physical size or conventional success—it's about the courage to treat your own thoughts and feelings and dreams as worthy of attention."

She looked directly at Jason Chen, who had been struggling with imposter syndrome in his first semester of college. "When you feel overwhelmed by the magnitude of what you're trying to become, remember that every important idea started small. Every breakthrough began with someone who was willing to take their tiny insight seriously enough to tend it and see what it grew into."

Jason's mother reached over and squeezed his hand, both of them recognizing wisdom that addressed exactly what they'd been discussing at home.

"The Realm of Emotion," Elsie continued, "showed me that feelings aren't weather that happens to you—they're tools you can learn to use consciously. I learned that fear often points toward what matters most to you, that anger can be fuel for necessary change, that even sadness serves a purpose when it helps you honor what was valuable about what you're leaving behind."

Am I being too abstract? Too weird? But Sophia is nodding, so maybe this is landing.

Sophia nodded vigorously, remembering their conversations about emotional literacy and the discussion group that had grown from their initial meeting.

"But here's what I discovered about applying that lesson in daily life," Elsie added, her voice growing warmer with the joy of sharing hard-won wisdom. "You don't need to visit impossible realms to practice using emotions as information. Every time you pause to ask what your anxiety might be trying to tell you instead of just trying to make it go away, you're doing the same work I did when the landscape dissolved under my feet. Every time you use your anger to identify what needs to change instead of just venting it or suppressing it, you're building bridges just as real as the ones that appeared in that magical place."

She told them about the Memory Orchard, where she'd learned to distinguish between honoring the past and being imprisoned by it, where she'd discovered that some promises could be kept even decades after they'd been made. Marcus Rivera wiped his eyes as she described how memories could be preserved as living things that continued to nourish rather than static recollections that trapped you in grief.

"The truth is," Elsie said, "we all have access to the Memory Orchard every time we choose to let gratitude for shared experiences fuel new adventures rather than using nostalgia as an excuse to stop growing. Every time we honor someone we've loved by becoming more rather than less, we're tending to memory fruit that continues to ripen with attention and care."

She described her encounter with her shadow self in the Archive of Inkless Names, but spoke about it in terms that everyone in the room could recognize—the internal voice that edits out possibility in favor of safety, that chooses certainty over growth, that would rather avoid disappointment than risk joy.

"I had to learn to negotiate with the part of myself that wanted to keep me small," she said, "to transform it from a harsh editor of my entire life into a wise counselor who helped me make thoughtful choices. That conversation is available to all of us. We all have internal voices that claim to be protecting us but are actually limiting us. The question isn't how to eliminate those voices—it's how to change the relationship so they serve growth rather than preventing it."

Several people in the audience were taking notes, recognizing descriptions of their own internal struggles with critical voices that made them feel like they weren't good enough, smart enough, brave enough to try for what they actually wanted.

When Elsie reached the part of her story about giving up the Atlas—choosing to trust her internalized growth rather than keeping access to external magic—the room grew so quiet she could hear the soft scratch of Kit's pen moving across paper.

"The hardest lesson," she said, "was learning that the magic was never in the book. It was never in the impossible realms or the fantastic creatures or the doorways that led to territories that couldn't exist on any ordinary map. The magic was in what those experiences taught me about my own capacity for transformation, my own ability to choose courage over comfort, growth over safety, the uncertain beauty of attempting over the certain emptiness of not trying."

This is the part where I either sound completely insane or somehow make sense. Please let it be the latter.

She looked around the room, making eye contact with faces that reflected varying degrees of recognition and hope and skeptical curiosity.

"I'm not telling you this story to convince you that magic exists in the form of enchanted books and impossible realms," she continued. "I'm telling it to suggest that magic exists in every moment when you choose to author your own story instead of letting fear do the writing, when you treat emotions as information rather than weather that happens to you, when you use uncertainty as a compass for navigation rather than a reason to stay put."

Mrs. Henderson raised her hand, and Elsie nodded encouragingly.

"But how do you start?" she asked. "How do you begin to live that way when you've spent years being careful and practical and sensible?"

The question I've been asking myself for most of my adult life.

Elsie smiled, recognizing the question she'd been asking herself for most of her adult life.

"You start small," she said. "You start by noticing one thing each day that you'd usually take for granted but that actually deserves wonder. You start by paying attention to one emotion each day and asking what information it might be trying to give you instead of just trying to feel better. You start by choosing one moment each day to act from curiosity instead of fear, from possibility instead of limitation."

She opened her Atlas to a page near the middle, where she'd been documenting the small experiments in conscious living that had become her daily practice.

"Three weeks ago," she read, "I noticed that every time I helped someone find exactly the book they needed, I felt a particular kind of joy that I'd been taking for granted. When I paid attention to that feeling, I realized it was telling me that I love being part of other people's discovery process. So I started asking patrons not just what they were looking for, but what they hoped to discover or understand or experience through reading. Those conversations have become some of the most meaningful parts of my day."

"Last month, I was feeling anxious about a budget meeting with the city council. Instead of just trying to manage the anxiety, I asked what it might be trying to tell me. I realized I was afraid that they wouldn't understand how vital the library is to our community's wellbeing. So I used that fear as motivation to prepare more thoroughly, to gather stories and statistics that demonstrated our impact rather than just hoping they'd see our value automatically. The meeting went better than any I'd had in years because I let my anxiety inform my preparation instead of just trying to ignore it."

She turned to a more recent entry.

"Yesterday, I was reading to the children's storytime group, and I noticed that one of the kids—a little girl who usually sits in the back and rarely speaks—was following along by moving her lips. Instead of just continuing with the planned program, I asked if she'd like to read a page out loud. It turned out she'd been practicing at home, hoping for exactly that opportunity. Her joy at being invited to participate changed the entire energy of storytime for everyone."

The examples were small, practical, accessible—proof that transformation didn't require dramatic gestures or impossible circumstances, just the willingness to approach ordinary moments with extraordinary attention.

"The magic," Elsie said, closing her Atlas and looking directly at her audience, "is learning to recognize that every day offers dozens of opportunities to choose growth over stagnation, connection over isolation, the interesting uncertainty of attempting something new over the boring certainty of staying exactly where you are."

A teenage girl in the back row raised her hand tentatively.

"What about when you try to do those things and it doesn't work out? What about when you choose possibility and it leads to failure or embarrassment?"

The question I've been afraid to ask for most of my life.

Elsie felt her heart expand with recognition of the question she'd been afraid to ask for most of her life.

"Then you have a story," she said simply. "Then you have evidence that you're someone who tries things, who takes risks in service of growth, who would rather have interesting failures than boring successes. Then you have material for the next experiment, information about what to try differently, proof that you're living fully enough to generate experiences worth learning from."

Kit looked up from their note-taking with an expression of pure pride and joy, recognizing the echo of conversations they'd had as children about the value of attempts over achievements.

"Besides," Elsie added with a smile that held all the mischief of someone who had learned to find adventure in the most ordinary circumstances, "some of the best discoveries come from experiments that don't turn out the way you expected. Some of the most interesting territories are only accessible through paths marked 'This Way Probably Won't Work, But It Might Teach You Something Worth Knowing.'"

The laughter that rippled through the room carried warmth and recognition and the particular relief that comes from being given permission to be imperfect while remaining courageous.

After the formal presentation ended, people lingered in the way that happens when a community discovers it has more in common than expected. Dr. Threadworth engaged Sophia in an animated discussion about the philosophical implications of emotional literacy. Marcus was showing Jason's mother photographs of the cooking classes he'd started for other widowed people, explaining how they'd become as much about community building as culinary skill development.

Mrs. Henderson approached Elsie with eyes bright with possibility.

"I've been thinking about what you said about starting small," she said. "About noticing one thing each day that deserves wonder. This morning I realized I've been taking my morning walks for granted—just thinking about them as exercise. But when I paid attention, I noticed how many different birds live in our neighborhood, how the light changes throughout the week, how many of my neighbors keep gardens that are works of art. It was like discovering I live in a more interesting place than I'd realized."

"That's exactly it," Elsie said with delight. "You're already doing the work. You're already exploring territories that were there all along, waiting for an explorer curious enough to notice them."

As the evening wound down and people began to leave, Kit approached Elsie with their notebook full of observations and insights from the evening.

"That was beautiful," they said. "Watching you share what you've learned, seeing how it landed with people who are hungry for exactly this kind of permission to live more consciously—it felt like watching magic happen in real time."

"What did you write?" Elsie asked, curious about Kit's documentation of the evening.

Kit flipped to the most recent entry and read aloud:

"December 18th. Witnessed Elsie Vine demonstrate the practical application of everything we learned as children about the possibility of living magical lives in ordinary circumstances. Watched forty-seven people remember that adventure is available to anyone willing to approach daily life with attention, intention, and the courage to choose growth over safety. Status: convinced that the most important explorations happen not in distant territories but in the conscious decision to live wherever you are with extraordinary presence."

Below the text, Kit had sketched a small map labeled "The Territory of Conscious Living," with landmarks like "The Valley of Daily Wonder," "The Mountains of Emotional Literacy," and "The River of Small Brave Choices."

"Perfect," Elsie said, recognizing the echo of their childhood cartography projects but updated with decades of wisdom about what kinds of territories were actually worth exploring.

As they prepared to close the library, Elsie looked around the space that had become so much more than her workplace. The comfortable reading chairs hosted conversations about transformation and growth. The shelves held books that found their way to exactly the people who needed them. The circulation desk had become a compass point where people could discover not just information but guidance toward the unexplored territories of their own possibilities.

From his terrarium, Minimus observed the evening's proceedings with satisfaction.

"Excellent demonstration of applied wisdom," he noted. "You've successfully transformed from someone who curated other people's stories into someone who actively helps others recognize they're the authors of adventures worth documenting."

"We all are," Elsie said, opening her Atlas to a fresh page. "Everyone who was here tonight, everyone who comes in tomorrow looking for books—they're all the protagonists of stories that haven't been fully written yet. The question is whether they'll have the courage to pick up the pen."

She began writing her documentation of the evening, but not just as a record of what had happened. As an invitation for whatever story wanted to unfold next, as evidence that transformation was always available to anyone willing to approach it with honesty and hope and the understanding that magic was not a destination to reach but a quality of attention to cultivate.

"December 18th," she wrote. *"Shared the story of transformation with forty-seven fellow explorers of the possible. Discovered that the most important adventures begin not when someone finds an enchanted atlas, but when they decide to treat their ordinary life as territory worth exploring with extraordinary attention. The door between transformation and daily life remains permanently open, because there was never a door at all—only the artificial boundary between who we think we are and who we're actually capable of becoming."*

Outside, the December evening painted Millbrook in shades of silver and possibility, and somewhere in Portland, Kit was driving home with a notebook full of observations about the evening and plans for implementing similar programs at Atlas Books and Curiosities.

The atlas on Elsie's desk—no longer magical in any supernatural sense, but filled with the accumulated evidence of a life consciously lived—lay open to pages that chronicled not just her own transformation but the ripple effects of choosing growth over safety, courage over comfort, the uncertain beauty of attempting over the certain emptiness of never trying.

The story was complete, but not finished. Could never be finished, because each day offered new opportunities for exploration, new territories of the self to discover, new ways of living that were more aligned with who she was becoming rather than who she had been afraid she would always remain.

The magic was real, more real than it had ever been when confined to impossible realms or dependent on enchanted objects. It lived in every moment when someone chose to author their own adventure, in every decision to treat uncertainty as information rather than threat, in every recognition that ordinary life could become extraordinary through the simple, radical act of paying attention to what was actually happening rather than what you feared might happen or wished were happening instead.

The librarian had found her answer: that the most important question was never whether magic existed, but whether you had the courage to create it through your choices, your attention, your willingness to live as if wonder were always available to those brave enough to look for it in exactly the place where they already were.

The adventure continued, would always continue, because transformation was not a destination but a practice, not an achievement but a commitment, not something that happened to you but something you chose, again and again, each time you decided to become the conscious author of whatever story wanted to be written next.

EPILOGUE: THE RETURN OF THE MAP
ONE YEAR LATER

The book appeared on a Tuesday, as extraordinary things often do—not because Tuesday holds any particular magic, but because it's the sort of day when people are paying just enough attention to notice something wonderful while still being distracted enough to believe it might have been there all along.

Sarah Chen found it while reshelving returns in the Portland Public Library, wedged between a travel guide to Iceland and a memoir about finding purpose after retirement. She might have dismissed it as a misfiled item, except for the way it seemed to pulse gently under her fingers, warm as if it had been sitting in sunlight, and the way the cover made her think of all the places she'd never been brave enough to visit.

Wait. Did this book just...?

The Atlas of Elsewhere, read the title in elegant script that seemed to shift slightly when she wasn't looking directly at it. Below that, in smaller letters: *A Guide to the Territories of the Heart.*

Sarah was twenty-six, had been working as a librarian for eight months, and had spent most of those months feeling like she was pretending to be someone competent while secretly being convinced that everyone else had figured out some essential truth about living that had somehow bypassed her entirely. She opened the book to the first page, expecting to find a table of contents or perhaps an introduction about geographical territories.

Instead, she found an inscription written in handwriting that looked both confident and kind:

For whoever needs the map next. The territories you'll explore already exist within you, waiting for someone brave enough to acknowledge that feeling lost is often the first step toward finding something worth discovering. The journey changes you, but only into who you were always capable of becoming. Trust the process. Trust yourself. Real explorers always find their way home.

—E.V.

Sarah felt something shift in her chest, a recognition she couldn't name but somehow understood perfectly. She turned the page and found herself looking at a map of an island shaped like a sleeping cat, labeled "The Realm of Scale" in that same elegant script.

The atlas murmured—not audibly, but in the way that books sometimes speak to the part of you that remembers what it felt like to believe in impossible things.

Okay, Sarah. You're either losing your mind or something very interesting is about to happen.

From her desk across the library, her supervisor Mrs. Martinez looked up from processing new acquisitions with the vague sense that something significant was happening near the travel section, though she couldn't have said what.

Sarah closed the atlas carefully, her hands trembling slightly with anticipation and terror and the particular excitement that comes from recognizing an invitation to adventure disguised as an ordinary Tuesday afternoon.

She checked the return slip tucked inside the front cover, expecting to find the name of whoever had donated it to the library's collection. Instead, she found an address written in that same confident script: *Atlas Books and Curiosities, 847 NW Glisan Street, Portland.*

That place I've been meaning to check out for months.

The bookstore was only twelve blocks away. Sarah had passed it dozens of times on her way to and from work, always meaning to explore its interesting window displays but somehow never quite finding the time. Now, holding the impossible atlas against her chest like armor or talisman, she realized that time wasn't something you found—it was something you created by choosing to step through doors that appeared when you were finally ready to walk toward them.

She approached Mrs. Martinez's desk with the careful composure of someone making a decision that might change everything.

"I need to take my lunch break," she said, her voice steady despite the way her heart was racing with possibilities she couldn't yet name.

"Of course, dear," Mrs. Martinez replied, and then paused, studying Sarah's face with the attention of someone who had been working with books and people long enough to recognize the signs of someone standing at the threshold of important change. "Take all the time you need."

Sarah walked through the Portland afternoon carrying the atlas and the growing conviction that some invitations, once received, required immediate response. The city looked different somehow— more alive with potential, more filled with doorways that might lead to territories she'd never imagined exploring.

Am I really doing this? Am I really following a mysterious book to a bookstore because it felt warm under my fingers?

Yes. Apparently I am.

At Atlas Books and Curiosities, she found a store that seemed to exist in the spaces between practical travel planning and impossible adventure, its shelves filled with guidebooks to real places and maps to territories that couldn't be found on any ordinary atlas. The owner, a person with ink-stained fingers and eyes the color of creek water, looked up from helping another customer with an expression of warm recognition.

"You found it," they said simply, as if they'd been expecting her.

"I found it," Sarah confirmed, though she wasn't entirely sure what she'd found beyond the growing certainty that her life was about to become significantly more interesting than she'd previously believed possible.

The atlas in her hands pulsed gently, ready for whatever journey wanted to unfold next, in whatever territories needed exploring by someone finally brave enough to trust that getting lost was often the most reliable path toward finding exactly where you belonged.

Across the country, in a library in Millbrook, Elsie Vine looked up from helping a patron find resources about starting over after major life changes, touched by the sudden, inexplicable certainty that somewhere, someone was about to discover what she had learned: that the most important maps were the ones that led not to places, but to the unexplored possibilities of becoming more fully yourself.

The atlas continued its eternal circulation, finding its way to exactly the people who needed exactly the lessons it was uniquely equipped to provide. It taught each traveler that courage was a choice, that wonder was always available, and that the most extraordinary adventures often began on the most ordinary Tuesday afternoons, when someone finally decided they were ready to become the author of their own impossible story.

POSTSCRIPT: THE PHILOSOPHERS' DEBATE

Somewhere very far away—and not far at all—the Inch-High Council was conducting its 3,847th annual debate, though this year's topic had taken an unexpectedly personal turn.

High Philosopher Threadbeard paced the acorn podium, his dandelion-fluff beard quivering with indignation. "She left without submitting a final report! No citations! No peer review! How are we supposed to catalog her findings in the Official Registry of Transformative Experiences?"

"She abandoned proper academic protocol," Professor Leafcloak agreed, adjusting her autumn maple cape with scholarly disapproval. "Departure without footnotes is practically barbarian."

Dr. Pebblestone cleared his throat from behind his stack of rice-grain-sized research notes. "Perhaps we're approaching this from the wrong angle. The Large One completed her thesis—just not in the format we expected."

"What thesis?" Professor Twigsnap demanded, nearly falling off her acorn podium in excitement. "Where are the appendices? The bibliography? The seventeen supporting arguments?"

"Her life," said a small voice from the corner.

They all turned to look at Professor Dewdrop, the council's youngest member, who rarely spoke during formal debates but had been taking copious notes in handwriting so tiny it required a magnifying glass to read a magnifying glass to decipher.

"Her life became the thesis," Dewdrop continued, gaining confidence. "She didn't write about transformation—she demonstrated it. She didn't theorize about courage—she practiced it. She didn't document the journey—she lived it."

Professor Leafcloak harrumphed. "That's terribly unscholarly. How do we cite lived experience in the Official Registry?"

"Besides," Threadbeard added, "she was supposed to return for the annual symposium on 'Unstable Realities and the Ethics of Snack-Based Diplomacy.' I had seventeen questions prepared!"

"You miss her," Professor Twigsnap observed with the bluntness that made her unpopular at faculty meetings. "She asked about your feelings, Threadbeard. No one else ever asks philosophers about feelings."

A moment of uncomfortable silence fell over the assembly, broken only by the scratch of Dr. Pebblestone's quill against parchment no larger than a flower petal.

"Very well," Threadbeard declared, attempting to restore academic dignity to the proceedings. "Today's emergency session will address the question: 'When the map ends, what writes the next line?'"

"Metaphorical cartography!" Professor Leafcloak sighed dreamily, her scholarly irritation immediately forgotten in favor of her favorite subject.

"Philosophical prattle," muttered Professor Thornwick. He had been hoping to debate something with more practical applications, like the aerodynamics of dandelion seeds.

"Breakfast-themed allegory!" shouted Professor Crumbcake, who had arrived late and was still covered in pollen from his morning constitutional through the nearby flower beds.

And so, beneath the vast curve of blue sky that stretched

endlessly above their tiny amphitheater, they began their debate with renewed enthusiasm. Arguments were made, counter-arguments offered, and sub-committees formed to explore the implications of cartographic metaphysics as applied to personal transformation.

During the first official break, refreshments consisted of nectar collected during particularly inspiring moments of philosophical discourse.

Professor Dewdrop approached the ancient chalkboard that dominated one wall of their meeting space. There, in Threadbeard's careful script, were still written the last known coordinates of Elsie Vine, along with detailed notes about her progress through various realms. But someone had recently added a line at the bottom in different handwriting:

"All who wander are updating the reference section."

"What do you suppose that means?" asked Professor Twigsnap, joining Dewdrop by the board.

"I think," Dewdrop said thoughtfully, "it means she's still exploring. Still discovering. Still adding to the sum total of what's known about courage and transformation and the willingness to author your own adventure."

"But how can she be updating the reference section if she's not here to file proper reports?"

Dr. Pebblestone approached, having overheard their conversation. "Perhaps the updating isn't happening in our library. Perhaps every choice she makes to live courageously, every moment she chooses growth over safety, every time she helps someone else discover their own capacity for transformation—perhaps all of that gets automatically catalogued in a reference section we don't have access to."

The idea sent ripples of excitement through the assembled philosophers. They immediately began constructing elaborate theoretical frameworks to explore the implications of distributed knowledge systems and the possibility that the most important discoveries might be recorded not in official registries but in the lived experiences of beings who had learned to navigate impossible territories.

As the afternoon sun painted their tiny world in shades of gold and possibility, Professor Threadbeard called for order.

"I move that we dedicate our next symposium to 'The Nature of Unfinished Journeys and Their Ongoing Contributions to Universal Knowledge.'"

"Seconded!"

"Thirded!"

"Motion to amend the title to include footnotes about snack-based diplomacy!"

The vote was inconclusive, as most of their votes tended to be. They would debate the motion for several more sessions before reaching a decision, which they would then debate for several sessions more.

But as they clinked their thimble-sized cups of honey-laced ink in a toast to unresolved questions and ongoing explorations, something remarkable happened. A gentle breeze stirred through their amphitheater, carrying with it a small piece of paper that hadn't been there moments before.

It was a map—not precise, not complete, but unmistakably drawn in Elsie's careful handwriting. It showed new territories she'd been exploring, marked with tiny X's at locations labeled "Tuesday Adventure," "Library Magic," "Kit's Bookstore," and "Home (Transformed)."

At the bottom, in letters small enough to be read by beings who specialized in the philosophy of scale, was a note:

"Thank you for teaching me that significance isn't about size, but about the courage to engage deeply with the mystery of existence itself. The journey continues. —E.V."

Professor Dewdrop carefully pinned the map to the bulletin board next to their official proceedings, where it fluttered gently in the afternoon breeze like a flag of ongoing possibility.

"Well," said High Philosopher Threadbeard, stroking his beard with satisfaction, "I suppose that settles the question of whether her journey was complete or ongoing."

"Does it?" asked Professor Leafcloak. "I think it raises seventeen new questions about the epistemological implications of cartographic correspondence."

"Wonderful!" Dr. Pebblestone exclaimed, already reaching for his note-taking materials. "We'll have enough material for the next century of debates."

And so the philosophers continued their eternal discussion, sustained by the joy of questions that mattered more than their answers, explorations that valued the journey over the destination, and the recognition that the most important adventures were available to beings of any size who approached existence with sufficient curiosity and wonder.

In their tiny amphitheater, surrounded by thoughts that had grown large enough to provide architecture for impossible conversations, they pursued their work with the satisfaction of knowing they had helped launch at least one consciousness from fear-based limitation to love-based expansion. And somewhere in the vast world beyond their realm, the ripples of that transformation continued to spread in ways they might never fully catalog, but would forever celebrate.

The questions would never be fully answered.

But that was exactly the point.

COMING NEXT IN THE SERIES

*The adventures continue in **The Archive of Unsaid Things**. When Elsie receives a letter that shouldn't exist, she and Kit discover a realm where bridges collapse under the weight of withheld truths and libraries hum with the silence of things never spoken. To escape, they must confront what they've left unsaid—even to each other.*

CHAPTER 1: THE LETTER THAT SHOULDN'T BE

The letter arrived on a Wednesday morning, which should have been the first sign that something was wrong. Kit always wrote on Sundays—part of their carefully negotiated correspondence schedule that had evolved over the six months since their reunion. Sunday letters from Portland, Thursday replies from Millbrook, with the comfortable rhythm of two people learning to be friends again across both distance and time.

But this letter felt different before Elsie even opened it. The envelope was the wrong color—not Kit's usual cream stationery, but something that seemed to shift between gray and silver depending on how the light caught it. Her name was written in handwriting that looked almost like Kit's, but somehow... hollow, as if the words had been traced rather than written with intention.

Most disturbing of all, the postmark was from a place that didn't exist: Silence, Oregon. Population: Unknown.

What the hell?

"That's peculiar," Minimus observed from his terrarium,

adjusting his tiny monocle to get a better look at the envelope. In the months since Elsie's return from the realms, he had become something of a postal critic, offering commentary on the emotional content of her correspondence before she'd even opened it. "The envelope appears to be resonating with frequencies I haven't encountered since your journey through the impossible territories."

Elsie turned the letter over in her hands, noting that it felt lighter than it should—not just physically light, but somehow *less present*, as if it existed only partially in the ordinary world.

This can't be good.

Inside, written on paper that seemed to absorb light rather than reflect it, was a message in Kit's handwriting that made her blood run cold:

Elsie,

By the time you read this, I'll probably be gone. Not dead—I need you to know that—but gone in a way that's harder to explain. I've been pulled into something I don't understand, a place where all the things we never said to each other have taken on a life of their own.

Do you remember when we were children, how we used to finish each other's sentences? How we could communicate without words, how we always knew what the other was thinking? I thought we still had that. I thought our reconnection was complete, that we'd said everything that mattered.

I was wrong.

There are things I never told you, Elsie. Important things. Things I was too afraid to say when we were sixteen, things I've been too careful to mention in our letters, things I've been editing out of our conversations because I was terrified of disrupting the perfect friendship we've rebuilt.

But unspoken truths have their own gravity, and mine have been growing heavier every day. Now they've pulled me into a place where silence has architecture, where the words we swallow become the walls that trap us.

If you get this letter—and I'm not sure how the postal system works between here and ordinary reality—please don't try to find me. I don't think it's safe for anyone else to enter this place. The Archive of Unsaid Things doesn't distinguish between comfortable silences and destructive secrets. It just collects them all, builds worlds from them, and traps the people who created them.

I should have told you I love you. Not just as a friend, though I do love you as a friend. But more than that. I should have told you that when we were sixteen, I didn't just miss you after we said goodbye—I grieved for you like a lost piece of my soul. I should have told you that every letter I wrote but never sent over the years was a love letter, in one form or another.

I should have told you that when we reunited, the joy I felt wasn't just about reclaiming a childhood friendship. It was about finding the person I'd been in love with my entire life and discovering that thirty years had only made you more beautiful, more wise, more everything I'd always known you could become.

But I didn't tell you any of that, because I was afraid it would change things between us, afraid you didn't feel the same way, afraid of risking what we'd just rebuilt.

Now those unspoken words have become a prison, and I'm paying the price for choosing silence over honesty.

Don't follow me, Elsie. Live your life. Write your stories. Help other people find their way to the truths they're brave enough to speak.

But know that in whatever realm I'm trapped in now, I'm still loving you with all the words I never found the courage to say.

Kit

P.S. - If you do something foolish like trying to rescue me (which would be exactly the kind of impossible thing you've learned to believe in), look for the door that opens onto silence. But please, please don't. Some mistakes are meant to be lived with, not corrected.

Elsie read the letter three times, each reading making her hands shake more violently. By the third time through, she was crying—not the gentle tears of recognition she'd shed during their reunion, but the raw, desperate sobs of someone watching everything good in their life slip away just as they'd learned to believe in it.

Oh, Kit. You beautiful idiot. Of course I felt the same way. Of course I've been editing myself too.

"This is my fault," she whispered to Minimus, who had been watching her read with growing alarm. "All those letters Kit wrote, all those visits where we talked about everything except... except this. I felt it too, but I was too afraid to name it. I was too careful, too worried about disrupting what we'd rebuilt."

We're both such cowards. Thirty years of friendship and we still can't say what we actually mean to each other.

"Perhaps," Minimus said gently, "the question isn't whose fault it is, but what you're going to do about it."

Elsie looked around her library, seeing it suddenly not as the transformed space where magic happened through conscious attention, but as the place where she'd learned that silence was sometimes the enemy of truth, that some things grew more dangerous when left unspoken.

She thought about Kit trapped in a realm built from withheld words, paying the price for both of their careful omissions. She thought about the love that had been growing between them—not just rekindled friendship, but something deeper and more complex —that neither of them had been brave enough to acknowledge.

We learned to be brave about everything except the thing that mattered most.

She thought about the choice between safety and growth, between comfortable lies and difficult truths, between the known territory of careful friendship and the unmapped landscape of vulnerable love.

"I have to go after them," she said, the decision crystallizing even as she spoke it. "I have to find the Archive of Unsaid Things."

"Even though Kit specifically asked you not to?"

"Especially because Kit asked me not to," Elsie replied, standing up and moving toward her desk with sudden purpose. "Because asking me not to follow is just another way of protecting me from risk instead of trusting me to make my own choices about what I'm willing to attempt."

And because if the situations were reversed, Kit would already be packing.

She opened her transformed Atlas to a fresh page and began writing, documenting her intention with the same careful attention she'd learned to bring to all her choices:

> *"March 23rd. Kit has been taken by the Archive of Unsaid Things, a realm built from the words we've been too afraid to speak. They asked me not to follow, but love isn't about respecting people's fears—it's about trusting their capacity to grow beyond them. I'm going to find them, and I'm going to say everything we've both been too careful to say. Some truths are too important to leave unspoken, even when speaking them means risking everything we've built together."*

As she wrote, something extraordinary happened. The words began to glow on the page, not with the warm light of memory or the silver shimmer of possibility, but with something new—the deep blue luminescence of truth that had been held back too long and was finally ready to be spoken.

A door began to appear on the blank wall of her office, sketching itself into existence with the slow inevitability of something that had been waiting to be opened.

Above it, words wrote themselves in script that looked like Kit's handwriting but felt like her own voice: *The Archive of Unsaid Things: Where Silence Has Architecture and Truth Builds Bridges.*

"Are you ready?" Minimus asked, settling himself more securely on her shoulder.

"No," Elsie said, moving toward the door that led to whatever realm had claimed the person she loved. "But I'm going anyway. Because some conversations are too important to leave unfinished, even when you're not sure how they'll end."

Especially when you're terrified of how they might end.

She reached for the door handle, carrying with her thirty years of unspoken words and the newfound courage to finally, finally say them all.

[Continue reading in The Archive of Unsaid Things...]

AUTHOR'S NOTE

The Atlas of Elsewhere was written for anyone who has ever wondered if it's too late to change course.

Elsie Vine's journey mirrors our own tangled paths—full of missed chances, quiet courage, and the magic of small things.

Whether you see yourself in the beetle, the mushroom poet, the star-masked guide, or just a slightly lost librarian— I hope this story reminds you that there's always a next chapter.

You don't have to finish everything.

You just have to begin again.

Keep wandering!

LJ

Want to stay connected? Visit the author's website for updates on future stories, behind-the-scenes notes, and bonus materials.

AUTHOR'S NOTE

https://WineGlassPress.com/books/the-atlas-of-elsewhere

ACKNOWLEDGMENTS

This book would not exist without the quiet spaces, strange dreams, and generous hearts that fueled its creation.

To every librarian who helped me learn how to search and find and search some more —thank you.

To my friends, mentors, and fellow wanderers—you helped me find the courage to map a world that didn't yet exist.

To you, dear reader, wherever you are: may your story always be worth rereading.

And to the Joy in my life. You know who you are ;-)

www.ingramcontent.com/pod-product-compliance
Lightning Source LLC
Chambersburg PA
CBHW060451300726